Quinny & Hopper

Written by Adriana Brad Schanen
Illustrated by Greg Swearingen

Los Angeles • New York

Printed in the United States of America

First Hardcover Edition, June 2014
First Paperback Edition, April 2015
10 9 8 7 6 5 4 3 2 1
J689-1817-1-15015
Library of Congress Control Number for Hardcover: 2013050369
ISBN 978-1-4847-1666-3

Visit www.DisneyBooks.com

For Glen, Madeline, and Julia.
And for my parents, whose big dreams
paved the way for mine. I love you.

One

Quinny

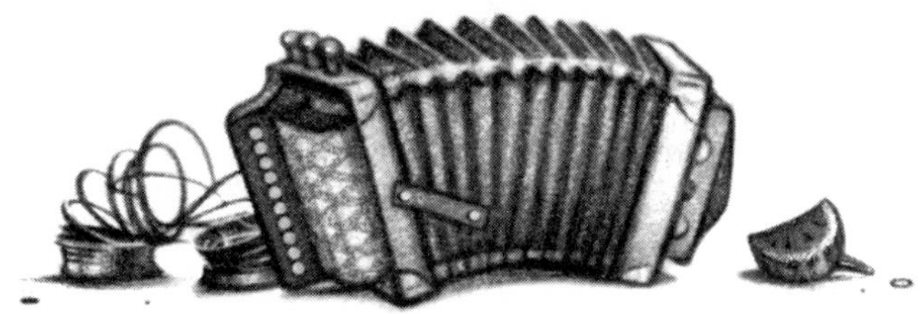

The moving truck is so tall that you have to climb up stairs to get into it. So I do.

Inside it's got a steering wheel as big as a hula hoop and tons of rocket-ship control panels and a bouncy driver's seat that's a trampoline just for my bottom. Plus the air in here smells warm and gooey, like pizza and cinnamon buns all squished together.

"Quinny Bumble, get down from there!" calls Mom from the sidewalk.

The good news is, in eight years I'll be old enough to drive this thing.

The grumpy news is, today we're moving.

We = me + Mom + Daddy + Pee-U Piper +

icky-sticky-screamy Cleo + 147 boxes of all our stuff.

Good-bye, New York City. Hello, some other place in the middle of nowhere that we have to go live for Mom's new job.

The list of things I'm going to miss about my city is very, very, extra-very long.

I'll miss climbing the wall of bookshelves in our apartment and saving Central Park snowballs in our freezer. I'll miss digging for buried treasure in the recycling closet down the hall and chatting in the lobby with our doorman, Paco. I'll miss riding my scooter through goopy green puddles at the curb and taking the train to school—underground!

I'll miss my friends the most. I've got friends from all nine floors of my building, from all three floors of my school, from theater camp, tap dance, tae kwon do, and accordion lessons. I've got friends from the farmers' market, the bagel store, the bookstore, the thrift store, and from just walking through Central Park.

"You'll make new friends and new lists when

we get to our new town," says Mom.

Baking cookies from scratch = fun.

Starting life from scratch = no fun.

Daddy won't even let me ride in the giant moving truck. He makes me squeeze into the backseat of our tiny car between Pee-U Piper, who's four and licks, and icky-sticky-screamy Cleo, who's one and bites. There's barely enough room back here for my mini-cooler, which fits just one precious Central Park snowball from our freezer. Plus did I mention that Piper picks her nose and Cleo farts so loud it sounds like she's got a tuba in her diaper?

We speed up onto the West Side Highway, zooming away from my fabulous city. We cross the George Washington Bridge, probably for the last time ever. I'm so sad thinking about it that I fall asleep. But

in the middle of my nap, Piper sticks a licky-wet finger in my ear. Deep, deep, deep into my warm, dry, sleepy ear. I wake up and howl, which makes Cleo wake up and howl, which makes Mom howl from the front seat: "Quinny, please!"

"Please what? She licked me again!"

But spit is see-through, so I never have any proof.

"Honey, she's just four," says Mom.

"When she's five, you'll say, 'She's just five.' When she's six, you'll say, 'She's just six.'"

I put my hand over Piper's face and squeeze, as a consequence for her inappropriate behavior.

"Quinny Bumble, that's enough!" Mom howls again.

"She started it!"

"Then be the one to finish it. You're the oldest, so set a good example."

Mom is always going on about this *setting an example* stuff. I'm sick of it. Just because I'm almost nine (which is the age in between eight-and-a-half and really, truly, absolutely nine) she expects me to be perfect. Why doesn't Mom make Piper set an example for Cleo? She's older than Cleo, after all!

It's going to be a long ride. Hours and hours long . . . hours of trying to stop Cleo from biting my hair . . . hours of playing Crazy Eights with Piper (who cheats) . . . hours of holding it in till the next gas station and belting it out to "Ob-La-Di, Ob-La-Da" by the Beatles (the most awesome band ever invented) . . . hours of staring out at nature, nature, and more nature . . .

I wait for all this nature to turn back into something interesting, like a subway stop or a skyscraper, but it doesn't. Finally, we pass a sign: WELCOME TO WHISPER VALLEY.

"This is it!" says Daddy.

"This is what?" I ask.

"Our new town," says Mom.

I look around. Whisper Valley has a million trees but no people. The houses don't even touch each other—no wonder they look so bored. I lower the car window. It's quiet out here, way too quiet. I sniff the air, which has exactly zero flavor.

"Look, here's the downtown!" says Mom. "Isn't it charming?"

There's not much *town* in Whisper Valley's downtown. You can practically see the whole thing with one eyeball.

Hardware store + deli + dry cleaners + pizza place < downtown.

"Where's the bagel store?"

"Not every town has a bagel store," says Daddy. "The deli here sells bagels."

"Where's the bookstore?"

"Quinny, please."

The sidewalk here looks so clean I don't think anyone ever walks on it. We drive by an empty train station. We drive by an empty playground. Where is everybody?

Finally the car stops—in front of a barn.

"This is it!" says Daddy.

"This is what?" I ask.

"Our new home," says Mom.

"We're moving into a barn?"

"It's not a barn," says Mom. "It's a house. It's called a Dutch Colonial. Isn't it lovely?"

I take another look. It's the shape of a barn. The color of a barn. "Are there cows and pigs inside?" I ask.

Mom rolls her eyes. She learned that from me.

Our new barn-house comes with new rules.

"No touching the rosebushes out front," says Daddy.

Ouch! Now I know why.

"No swinging on the porch swing," says Mom.

No fair. It's not called a *porch sit-still-and-be-bored*, is it?

"No riding your scooter around the living room," says Daddy.

Why not? This place is huge.

"We finally have room for a dog!" I call out. "Let's go to the shelter and pick one out!"

"Quinny, please," answers more grown-up groaning. "Go check out your new room."

My new room is up eleven creaky stairs and down an ultralong hallway that's perfect for bowling. It's got one squeaky door, two sunny windows, a closet that smells like Grandma's hugs, and a ceiling that looks like coconut frosting. (I don't know if it tastes like coconut frosting, because it's too high up to lick. I'm going to need a ladder.)

The good news about having my own room is I won't have to smell Piper's pee-u when she doesn't wake up in time to run to the bathroom at night. Plus I can decorate this place any way I want. My favorite paint color is a tie between green with orange polka dots and orange with green polka dots. Maybe I'll even put in a porch swing.

The grumpy news about having my own room is it's kind of lonely in here. How will I fall asleep at night without Piper's snoring? How will I wake up without her hunting for boogers up my nose with a flashlight?

"Time for lunch," Daddy calls from outside.

My parents unpack a picnic in our new back-yard. Mom hands out sandwiches to everyone except Cleo (who has to eat soft-serve peas because she doesn't have any teeth yet).

"Isn't this beautiful?" says Daddy.

"I guess. If you like trees."

"Quinny, what's gotten into you? You loved Central Park, and it was full of trees."

"But Central Park had other stuff, too."

It had crazy-bright Rollerbladers and freaky-fast bikers and zoomy runners. It had singers and guitar players and picture-painters in wacky outfits. It had dogs galore and a whole zoo, even, plus a skating rink, a puppet theater, and a giant pond. Our new yard has just us in it. And all the yards around us are empty. Where is everybody?

Finally something happens. A chicken hops by. A real, live chicken, just like the kind you hear about in books. Except this one's stylish—it's got black and white stripes, like a zebra.

I knew this house was really a barn!

"Mom, Daddy, look!"

But Mom's busy trying to get Piper down from a tree. Daddy's busy changing Cleo's stinky diaper and wiping her screamy spit-up from his glasses at the same time.

If I'm going to catch us a pet, I've got to think fast. So I follow that zebra-chicken and try to introduce myself. It hops over to the back of my house and *BOCK BOCK BOCK*s at the kitchen door, like it's angry about something.

"Hi there, chicken, I'm Quinny. Come inside and make yourself at home!"

The chicken turns and glare-stares at me, like I've done something wrong. Then it runs off.

"Hey, chicken! Come back, I don't bite!"

It races into another yard. I keep following it. And following it. Until it's gone.

Uh-oh.

Now, where am I? And what's that over there—a swing set? And who's on it? I can't see through all this nature. Maybe it's a girl. Maybe she's almost nine, too. Or maybe it's a boy. A friendly boy who likes to climb bookshelves and collect snowballs. I run over to find out.

Uh-oh again. That's not a swing set—it's a fence around a garden. A garden full of strange tomatoes. Yellow, orange, purple, green tomatoes . . . big and small and smooth and lumpy-bumpy tomatoes . . . even heart-shaped tomatoes, which I've never seen before in my life.

And the person inside this garden is definitely not a kid.

"Excuse me, young lady!" says an old lady, crouching and digging in the dirt.

"You are excused," I say. "Did you happen to see a chicken run by here?"

The old lady stands up. Way, way up. I've never seen a person so old and so tall both at the same time. She stares down at me, all serious and suspicious. I wonder if she knows she looks just like that guy on the front of my two-dollar bill.

"What about kids?" I try again, all smiley-polite. "Have you seen any kids around here?"

"I'm looking at one right now, and it's trespassing. This yard is private property."

"Oh. Sorry, I didn't realize. Back home, the outdoors belong to everyone."

"Where exactly do you live, young lady?"

I'm about to say New York City. But then I remember it's not true anymore. So I tell her, "In that house that looks like a barn, I guess."

That's all it takes. The giant old lady starts walking me right back to the big red barn-house.

"Can I ask you a question?" I ask her.

"If you must."

"Does anything exciting ever happen around here?"

"Rarely."

"That's what I was afraid of."

"Young lady, didn't anyone ever tell you not to talk to strangers?"

"Then how would I ever meet anyone new?"

All of a sudden I hear some very familiar yelling.

"Quinny! Quinny?" says the yelling. "Quinny Bumble! Where are you?"

"I take it you are Quinny Bumble," says the old lady.

I nod.

"Well, I'm Mrs. Porridge."

I wonder if she knows she is named after yucky soup.

"And that chicken's name is Freya. Stay away from her. She almost killed my cat."

My ears perk up. A killer chicken? Now, that's exciting! And I didn't know Mrs. Porridge even had a cat. "You're so lucky to have a pet!" I tell her. "I was supposed to get a puppy once, but then I got my baby sister, Cleo, instead. What's your cat's name? Does it do any tricks? Can I come over and play with it? I'm free right now!"

But before Mrs. Porridge can answer me, we're back at the barn-house.

Mom makes a serious-stiff face at me. Daddy looks half carsick and half relieved.

"We were so worried," Mom says.

"Quinny, you know better than to run off by yourself," Daddy says.

I do. But sometimes I forget stuff I already know.

"I'm sorry," I tell them. Very, very, extra-very sorry.

My parents thank Mrs. Porridge. Then they give me a big talk about not running off by myself. Then they send me up to my room. By myself.

I trudge up the stairs, all slumpy and sad. Pee-U Piper is up here in the hall, smirky-smiling. Nothing makes her happier than when I'm in trouble. She's also holding my snowball

cooler—which reminds me I forgot to put that snowball in the freezer!

She hands me the cooler and says, "Ha-ha, your snowball gotted all melty."

"*Gotted* is not a word!" I grab that cooler and slam my door in Piper's face.

Then I sit there, all alone in my lonely new room. No pet chicken, no new friends, no nothing. Just a cooler, dripping dead snowball onto my feet.

Moving here was the grumpiest idea ever.

Two

Hopper

Making a foot is not easy.

That's because a human foot has twenty-six bones in it. Some are as tiny as a screw. I spread them all out on my bed. I start by connecting the calcaneus to the cuboid.

"Hopper Benjamin Grey!" calls Mom from downstairs. "Let's go!"

I connect the cuboid to the fifth metatarsals.

Our minivan's horn beeps.

"Come on!" calls Dad from the driveway. "We're late."

I put my foot bones back into their box. I slide the box under my bed and walk downstairs.

Aunt LuAnne's barbecue party is today. That means we all have to go to it.

In the front seat of the minivan, my parents joke and laugh.

In the middle seat, my big brothers, Trevor and Ty, shove each other.

In the back, I sit by myself and look out the window. Freya, the stray chicken, is eating from our songbird feeder again. I don't think she knows who she really is.

We get to Aunt LuAnne's party. She pushes her big, mushy face down to mine and kisses me hello with orange lipstink. "Cheer up, Hopper! Your cousins are here!" she booms up my nose.

Dad rubs my hair, hard. "Go on, have fun!"

He means his kind of fun. I try my best, but I'm no good at his kind of fun. The yard is crowded. And hot. Everybody here is talking at the same time. Some people are shouting, for no good reason. Some people are laughing, even though nothing funny is happening.

Trevor and Ty run around with a bunch of

giant middle-school cousins. They knock things over. They almost knock me over.

Cousin Ally finds me. She wants to paint a daisy on my cheek.

I dodge her paintbrush and get in line at a long table of food. The coleslaw is warm and soupy. The hamburgers are black and burnt. The bowl of potato chips is down to crummy bits.

But there's one hot dog left. And plenty of pickles.

I fix myself a plate and look for a place to sit. All the spots in the shade are taken.

Cousin Max wobbles over to me. He's two. He steals my hot dog, drops it, and screams.

"Hopper, please be nice to him!" says Mom, coming over to us. "Max is just a baby."

Actually, he's a toddler, but it's not worth arguing about. The outside of my head feels soggy from the hot sun. The inside of my head feels scratchy from all the crowded-party noise.

A flying Frisbee bonks me on the ear, and some girl cousins laugh.

Things aren't going well for me at Aunt

LuAnne's barbecue party. There's nobody here my age. There's nobody here my style. But if I try to stay alone, a grown-up will stop me. Already I see Dad across the yard, pushing Trevor and Ty to come over here and "include" me, which in their brains means "hit."

My brothers walk toward me, smiling now. The problem is, Trevor and Ty are twins. This means that whenever Trevor flips me upside down, Ty helps. And whenever Ty pounds me into the ground, Trevor helps. They're a team.

And they're getting closer.

If I stay put, I'll be dead meat. If I run, they'll chase me.

Then I notice that nobody is sitting underneath that long table of food.

Yet.

Sometimes it is easier to be with people's feet than people's faces.

It's quiet here under the table. No one rubs my head like I'm a puppy or forces me to have their kind of loud, hurting fun. I eat my pickle. I eat my empty hot dog bun.

Then a hand lifts the tablecloth.

"Hopper, why don't you come play in the sandbox," says Mom.

Because I'm eight years old, that's why.

"Hopper, why don't you come hang out with Grandpa Gooley," says Dad, right behind Mom. "He just got here."

I look over and see Grandpa Gooley giving piggyback rides to the little kids. After a while, he can't stand up straight. So I sit with him in the shade.

"Hopper, I know exactly how you feel," he says with a sigh.

I'm not sure exactly how I feel. I wonder how Grandpa Gooley could know. At least he doesn't tell me to cheer up.

I'm relieved when it's time to leave Aunt LuAnne's barbecue party.

Back home, I climb the stairs, two at a time. I push open the door to my room.

I pull the box out from underneath my bed and get back to work connecting foot bones. I connect the calcaneus to the talus. I connect the talus to the

navicular. Everything clicks into place.

My room is my favorite place in the world.

In my room, I feel calm enough to juggle. I feel relaxed enough to draw. I can have my regular personality in here and nobody will say, "Cheer up, Hopper!" I can feed my fish and put together body-part models. I can look at my favorite science book, *Atlas of Human Anatomy* by Frank H. Netter. (Grandpa Gooley gave it to me for my eighth birthday. It's the best and biggest picture book of body parts ever—real doctors even use it.)

In my room, I can be quiet without people thinking that it means I'm sad.

But today, just as I'm connecting the navicular to the cuneiforms, all my quiet stops.

A squeaky noise replaces it. It's coming from outside my window.

I go over to the window and peek outside. My muscles freeze. My breath gets stuck in my throat. Because there's someone out there, waving at me. Squeaking at me.

It's a girl.

And boy, she's got a lot of words in her mouth.

Three

Quinny

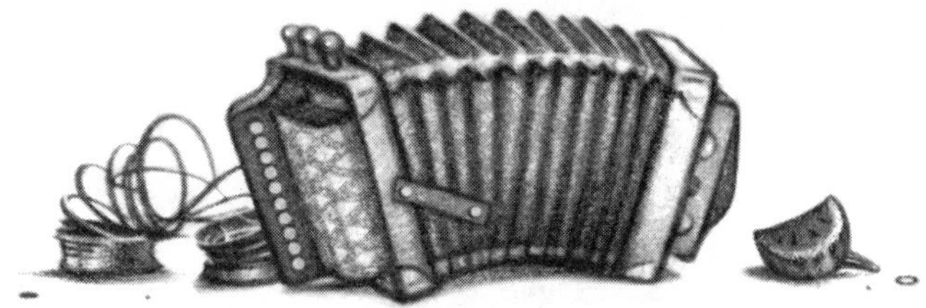

I'm so busy pouting on my bed that I don't even notice him at first. But then I look out my window and there he is, right past the trees, right inside the house next door. . . .

A boy! And he's kind of almost just about my size!

But the boy doesn't notice me back. So I open my window and holler, "Hey! Yoo-hoo! Over here! Hello? Hi there! How are you? I'm Quinny! Quinny Bumble! I just moved here from New York and I'm almost nine and my ceiling looks like coconut frosting! Who are you?"

Four

Hopper

I was afraid this would happen.

When Mr. McSoren moved out of the house next door, I knew somebody else would probably move in. That house is pretty big for just one person, so I figured it might be a group of people. A family.

I wonder how many of them there are. I hope they're not all as loud as this one.

Five

Quinny

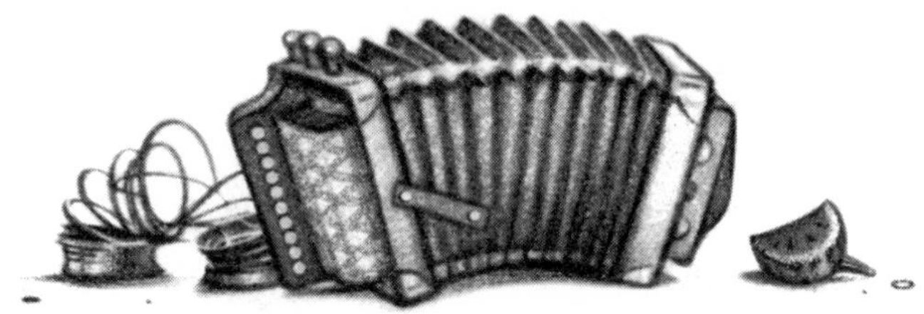

The boy stares back at me like he's never seen a girl before.

I'm about to keep talking to him, but then I hear Daddy's knuckles knock on my door.

"Daddy, come look! There's a boy next door, a real, live boy!" I yank him over to my window, but that boy is gone. "He was there! He really was—honest!"

"I believe you, Quinny," says Daddy. "His name is Hopper."

"It is?"

"His mother just came by to welcome us."

"She did?"

"She was also wondering if you wanted to go over there and meet Hopper."

I jump up so fast that I almost fall down—the answer is YES!

We hurry next door. Hopper's house looks just like the gingerbread house I decorated in school last year. He's lucky he gets to live in a tasty dessert house, not a stinky red barn-house.

Hopper's mom welcomes us in and starts talking to Daddy, and I wait for Hopper to start talking to me, too. But he just stands there, hiding behind his scruffy hair and peeking out at me with two big looking-looking eyes. His forehead is crinkled and his mouth is tiny, and I can tell he is trying to be brave. I can tell it is not working.

I know with shy dogs you are supposed to move slowly and speak gently and let them sniff your hand first. Same with shy humans, except for the sniffing.

"Hi, Hopper, remember me? I'm Quinny. We just met in our rooms, and I'm very, very, extra-very glad to meet you again, even though you're shy. I'm not shy, but some people are, and that's okay. I'm just excited you live next door and you're not as old as Mrs. Porridge!"

Hopper stares at me. His mom pushes him forward a little. "I'm Hopper," he says, barely.

Then he stares at something on my head that isn't my eyes. "Is that your real hair?"

"It is," I tell him. "My mom thinks it's beautiful."

Hopper doesn't say if he agrees with Mom or not. A lump bumps up in my throat.

"You do have fabulous hair, Quinny," says Hopper's mom. "Hopper, would you like to show Quinny your room?"

Hopper doesn't answer, but his mom pushes him along. I follow him upstairs and almost crash into him as he stops suddenly by a closed door. He blocks that door with his whole body.

Then he stares at my head again. "What are those holes in your cheeks?" he asks.

Another lump bumps up in my throat. "What holes?" I ask.

But Hopper doesn't explain. The next thing he says is, "How many teeth do you have?"

I don't know. But that's a good question. So I open my mouth and we count them.

Number of teeth in my mouth = 22.

Then we count Hopper's teeth.

Number of teeth in Hopper's mouth = 22, too!

"Oh, wow, Hopper, we have the exact same number of teeth! How cool is that! Do you have any loose ones? I still have two wiggly ones that are almost about to fall out—"

"Please don't shout so loud up my nose," Hopper says.

"Sorry." I step back an inch. "Is that better?"

Hopper doesn't answer this question. So I ask another one.

"What's behind that door you're blocking?"

"Body parts!" answers somebody else.

It's a big boy talking now—a bulky, bully-faced boy holding a soccer ball as he stomps down the hall toward us. He bounces that ball off Hopper's forehead. Ouch. Then a second bully boy, with the exact same face as the first one, shows up and shoves Hopper's shoulder. "Dead, rotting body parts." He snorts, sneering at me. "I wouldn't go in there if I were you."

"Well, you're not me," I say. "Now, could you please stop bothering my friend?"

"Your what?" Both bully boys laugh. They bounce that ball off Hopper's head again.

"My friend," I repeat. "And how would you like it if someone threw a ball at your face?"

"Hopper has a girlfriend! Hopper has a girlfriend!"

Those bullies make kissy-poo noises and mean laughing snorts. Then they grab Hopper and flip him upside down and swing him around. He doesn't look too happy about it.

"Leave him alone!" I pound a big bully arm and push a big bully stomach, but this two-headed bully monster swats me away like I am just some pesky little girl.

Well, I am *not* just some pesky little girl. Those bullyheads don't realize it, but I am a tae kwon do green belt. They have no idea what I had to *do* to earn that green belt. (Believe me, it was not pretty.) If they knew, they would be afraid. Very, very, extra-very afraid.

I get into my fighting stance. I pretend I am back at my *dojang* in New York City.

I front-kick a strong, fast foot, and I scream my spirit scream, "KEEEE-YAAAP!"

And *thwwwack*!

I kick that soccer ball right out of bullyhead #1's arms, and it flies high through the air. . . .

And down the hall.

And down the stairs.

Then I hear the crash and smash of something hard breaking into a million pieces.

Uh-oh. The

louder something sounds when it breaks, the more expensive it usually is.

That two-headed bully monster lets go of Hopper and glares down at me with fireballs of meanness shooting out of its four eyeballs.

"You're gonna get it!" growls bullyhead #1.

"You're dead meat!" snarls bullyhead #2.

"Wrong! I'll scream like a scared little baby, and you'll be the ones in trouble!"

"Quinny, what's going on here?"

I turn around. It's Daddy. He looks at me, half confused and half suspicious.

Hopper's mom rushes up the stairs behind Daddy, and she cries, "Trevor? Ty? Your grandmother's vase is broken! How many times have I told you: no playing ball in the house!"

"We didn't!" roars bullyhead #1.

"That girl broke it!" roars bullyhead #2. "She kicked the ball right out of my arms!"

Everyone looks at me. I try to smile, all sweet and innocent. Just a harmless little girl.

But there's one problem: Pee-U Piper.

I have no idea how she even got here, but my four-year-old twit-ster is suddenly sitting on the stairs, and she squawks, "It's true! Quinny hitted those boys and kicked their ball!"

That sneaky little thing was spying on me this whole time.

"*Hitted* is not a word," I point out.

"I sawed the whole thing," she says.

"*Sawed* isn't a word, either. Learn to speak English!"

"Quinny, please," says Daddy. "Is it true? Did you kick that ball down the stairs?"

"No! And even if I did, it was only because those big bullies made kissy-poo noises and tried to scare me with dead, rotting body parts, and then they turned Hopper upside down and—"

Daddy tries to interrupt me, but my engine is running too fast to stop.

"And they wouldn't cut it out, so I had no choice, because the *sabom* at my *dojang* always says we need to build a better, more peaceful world, which means you shouldn't hold people upside down by their ankles and spin them around without their permission, right?"

Hopper's mom looks totally confused now. So I fill her in.

"I happen to be a tae kwon do green belt, which is the belt right after yellow with a green stripe, and right before green with a blue stripe. For my belt test I broke a giant, thick piece of wood in two with just my bare foot."

I show Hopper's mom a strong, elegant side kick. She moves out of my foot's way.

"That's . . . well, that's very interesting, Quinny," she says. "Thank you for sharing."

"I'm sorry about your vase," I also share.

Daddy tells Hopper's mom that we will pay

for the vase. I don't know why, because none of this was my fault in the first place.

Hopper's mom says that is "out of the question," and then she turns to her own kids and says, "Boys, I'm disappointed in you. All three of you. This isn't how we behave with guests. You'll spend the rest of the afternoon in your rooms, thinking about how to use better manners."

"What?" wails bullyhead #1.

"No fair!" howls bullyhead #2.

Hopper's the only one who doesn't look upset to be stuck in his room for the rest of the day. I don't understand that boy.

"To your rooms—now!" Hopper's mom says. "And no video games, either."

The bully twins glare at me with tiny-meany eyes. One of them growls and the other whisper-shouts, "Dead meat!"

I stick close to Daddy, who's a lot bigger than they are. He picks up Piper and pulls me toward the stairs by my shirtsleeve. "Let's go, girls." His voice sounds like it has a headache.

“Bye, Hopper.” I wave back at him with a smile. “See you soon!”

But Hopper doesn’t wave or smile or say anything. He scowls at me like I’ve got cooties. Then he scurries into his room and slams the door.

I guess he hates me now, for some reason. I guess I didn’t make a new friend after all. As we walk away from Hopper’s house, Piper makes that smirky-sneaky smile that she always makes when I’m in trouble.

“Tattletale for sale!” I call out. “Tattletale for sale!”

“Quinny, please,” Daddy sighs. “I can’t believe what happened back there.”

“Neither can I.”

“You’ll help to pay for that broken vase out of your allowance.”

“But it wasn’t my fault! I was just standing there, doing my own life, when those bullies started bugging Hopper, so I tried to help him because I thought he was my friend. But I was wrong—he’s not my friend. That boy hates me, which is fine because it's a free country, so let's just move on, shall we?"

There's a sniffle in my nose, but I'm not letting it out for some boy who hates me.

Not. Going. To. Happen.

Six

Hopper

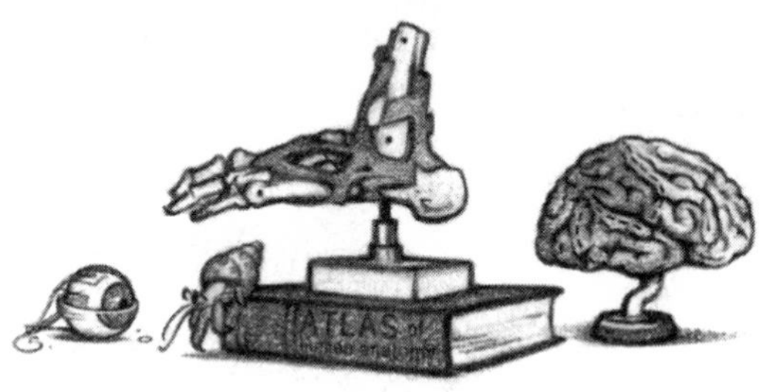

I watch Quinny walk away from my house. The back of her head, I notice, is much quieter than the front.

I watch the back of her head until she's gone. Then I pull down my window shade and get back to work on my foot model. I finish connecting the five metatarsals to the fourteen phalanges, which are the toe bones. These are tiny. These are tricky. (And they're more important than they look. Without all your toes, you would lose your balance when you walked.)

After a while, I go back to my window. I move the shade an inch and peek out.

Quinny's still gone. I'm glad about that. But I'm also sad she's not here anymore.

"Hopper?"

It's Mom. She touches my shoulder.

"You hungry?"

I shake my head.

"Trevor and Ty are playing downstairs."

That's a hint that the punishment is over and I'm allowed to leave my room, too. But I can hear what my brothers are doing downstairs. They are playing that video game where you explode the bad guy's head into drippy brain soup. This does not put them in a calm mood.

"I think I should stay in here and keep thinking about how to use better manners."

Mom doesn't fall for this.

She sits with me. "How are you doing on that foot?"

I show her what I've done so far. She tries to seem interested.

Then I say, "Quinny had big feet."

"Did she?"

She did. And big eyes. Big hair. And that big mouth, full of words.

Suddenly, I feel strange.

"Hopper, what's wrong?" Mom asks.

Something. But I don't know how to say it in sentences.

"Well, guess what, sweetie? Grandpa Gooley called to say he's going for a late swim tonight. Why don't you join him?"

Grandpa Gooley comes over, and we ride our bikes to the town pool. Just the two of us.

The only other person in the pool is my neighbor Mrs. Porridge. She's got on a swim cap that looks like bright parrot feathers, and she's doing the sidestroke. I wave. She waves back. The good thing about Mrs. Porridge is, she doesn't expect me to act louder than I really am.

I like the pool at night, when it's not crowded. I like swimming long and fast, which is called "swimming laps." Tonight I can swim laps without Trevor pulling my foot or Ty kicking my head.

I dive in. I hold my breath and swim underwater almost the whole way to the other end of the pool. Underwater is my second-favorite place in the world. When I'm swimming, I forget about stuff that's bugging me.

But when I'm done swimming, I remember it again.

"Hopper, is everything okay?" asks Grandpa Gooley as we dry ourselves off.

I don't know. So I don't answer. I'm glad it's getting dark out so he can't see my face, which feels hot all of a sudden.

"You're all tuckered out, aren't you?" he says. "Let's get you to bed."

Grandpa Gooley and I ride our bikes home. As we pull into my driveway, I look over at Mr. McSoren's old house, which is now Quinny's new house. Some of the lights are on. Some of the windows are open. People are talking and laughing in there. Someone's playing the accordion.

I look the other way. I try to listen the other way, too.

At bedtime, I brush my teeth. I floss my teeth. I think about Quinny's teeth. They were the happiest teeth I've ever seen.

But I wish she didn't have so many words in her mouth.

I wish she didn't shout all those words right up my nose.

I wish I had another chance to be her friend.

Seven

Quinny

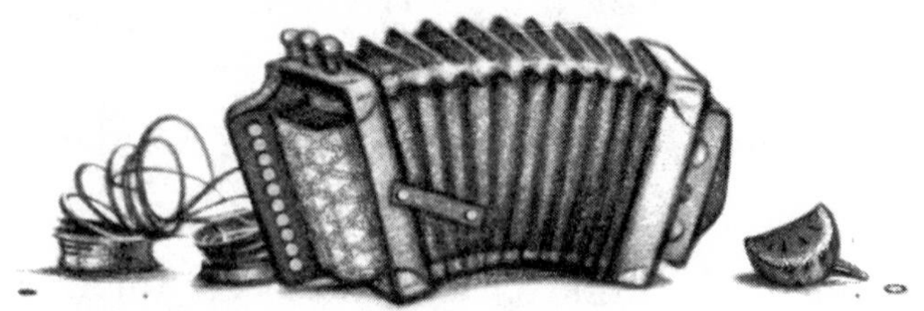

Pizza, if you're lucky enough to get some, is usually the best part of the day. But when Daddy opens up the box he just brought home from Whisper Valley Pizzeria, I gasp in disgust.

"Oh no! Can't this town do anything right?"

"Quinny, what's wrong? You love pizza."

"Not when it's cut up into a tic-tac-toe grid."

Square pizza = school cafeteria pizza. Real pizza comes in triangles. At least it did in New York City, where I wish we still lived.

I make a ferocious face at that yucky square pizza.

"Quinny, calm your engine down and eat your dinner," says Mom.

Instead, I rev my engine up and zoom away from the table and upstairs to my new room. Everything here is different. Everything here is awful. I hate Mom's new job for making us move to Whisper Valley. I hate this too-big house in this too-small town. I hate the clean sidewalks and the empty playground and the square pizza. I hate that two-headed bully monster Trevor/Ty and un-fun, un-friendly Hopper, who was rude to my interesting hair and wouldn't even let me in his room.

I just . . . hate.

Daddy comes upstairs. "I'm not hungry, so don't bother trying to feed me!" I inform him.

"Got it," he says. "Boy, it's been a crazy day, hasn't it?"

Daddy unpacks my suitcase and finds my pj's and sheets. We make up my bed together.

"I'll never find a friend here," I tell him.

"Never is a long time, Quinny."

"Exactly! That's why I'm sad. Why did we have to move here in the first place?"

"Honey, we talked about this. Mom got that

great job offer. And we wanted a house, a yard, a slower pace of life for our family. We wanted some peace and quiet—"

"Then we shouldn't have brought Cleo and Piper with us."

"Good point." Daddy smiles. "But I think we're stuck with them."

"Plus did you know that those giant bully twins next door are going to kill me? That's not very peaceful. Let's move back home before that happens, okay?"

"Honey, this *is* our home now. And nobody is going to kill you, I promise."

I can hear Mom playing the accordion in another room. Sometimes that's the only thing that gets Cleo to sleep.

"Let's give this place a chance." Daddy keeps talking. "It's the middle of July. I bet lots of families are away on summer vacation now. When school starts, you'll meet plenty of kids."

School? School won't start until September. That's practically forever from now.

Daddy kisses me good night. "Get some rest and you'll feel better in the morning."

I doubt it.

I lie there in bed and wait for Piper to barge into my room because she's scared of sleeping by herself. But she doesn't. I wait some more, in the quiet, empty dark. I'm not a big old baby-pants who needs to snuggle with anyone, that's for sure.

I close my eyes. My body is tired, but my head feels too thinky to sleep. I think about that stylish killer zebra-chicken named Freya I didn't get to pet, plus that boy named Hopper I didn't get to be friends with. I think about Hopper's crinkly forehead and his careful, quiet mouth and his soft, scruffy hair. I think about his looking-looking eyes, and how my heart did a little hop when he looked at me, and then a little flop when he slam-bam shut his door in my face. Making friends was a lot easier back in the city. Back home, there were so many kids to choose from. There were loud places to go and busy things to do, and I always ran into someone friendly.

Then I remember something. There is a train station in this too-small, too-quiet town. We drove by it today, and it isn't too far from my barn-house. In fact, I could probably walk there if I put my shoes on. So I make a decision: I'm moving back home, to my old building in New York City. It's the only place I will ever be happy.

I get up and dig around moving box #67 and pull out my puppy bank. I'm sure I have enough money in here for a train ticket. (Almost sure.) I'm sure Paco, the doorman in my old building, will let me sleep in the bike room. (Almost sure.) I'll sneak a slice or two from the pizza boxes that get delivered to the building every day. I'll read newspapers or magazines from the recycling instead of going to school. Sure, my parents might be a little sad at first, but they'll still have Piper and Cleo to keep them busy, and they can visit me anytime they're in the city.

I unzip my suitcase and stuff back in the clothes that Daddy just unpacked.

Then I pop open my puppy bank's belly button and pour out my money.

Eight

Hopper

At bedtime, I read to myself (chapters four and five of *The Bat-Poet*).

Then I read to Mom (*Goodnight Moon*, still her secret favorite).

Then it's time for one last hug.

She's about to turn off the light when I ask her, "Mom, what do you call those holes in Quinny's cheeks?"

"Holes?"

"When she smiled, there was a tiny hole here, and here." I point to the sides of my mouth.

Mom smiles. "You mean her dimples. They're part of what makes Quinny unique, aren't they?"

They are. I can't believe there's a body part I forgot about. Dimples.

Then Mom suggests we invite Quinny over to play again. Just me and her this time. Kind of like a fresh start.

I think about Mom's idea. But three questions happen inside my head.

What if Quinny says no?

What if Quinny says yes?

What if Trevor and Ty tease me again about playing with a girl?

Mom must be a mind reader, because the next thing she says to me is: "Hopper, the most interesting boys play with both boys and girls. And besides, you are practically an expert at ignoring Trevor and Ty when they tease."

She's right about that. I feel a little better.

"Can we call her right now?" I ask.

"It's late," says Mom. "Let's wait until morning. Quinny isn't going anywhere."

But morning is eight hours away. That's a long time to let a person think I'm not nice. I didn't even say bye to Quinny. She has no idea how much I like her teeth.

I go to bed. But not to sleep.

And then I find an idea of my own. A big one.

I go over to my desk. I get out my set of charcoal pencils, the kind that real artists use.

I get out my sketch pad.

Sometimes it's easier to draw how you feel than to say how you feel.

Nine

Quinny

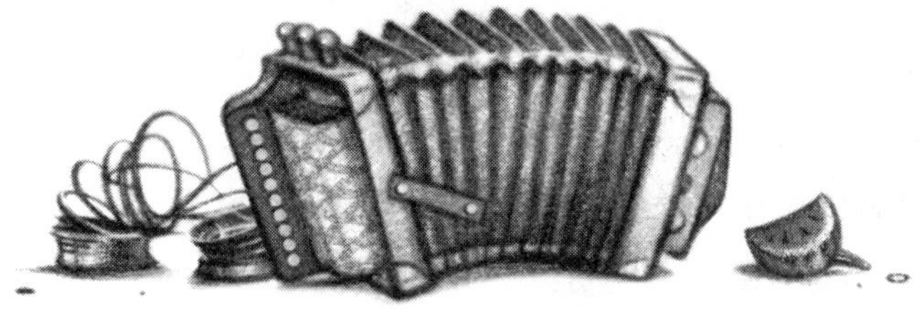

I stuff my pockets full of money and my suitcase full of clothes and my sneakers full of feet and my head full of courage. I'm going to need all the courage I can get because it's dark outside. I look out my window again—very, very, extra-very dark. The streetlamps in Whisper Valley don't work too well, I guess.

I wonder what nature is like at night. I hope that killer chicken doesn't attack kids. A lump bumps up in my throat, but I swallow it. I will be fine once I get to the train station. It's still there, I hope. Train stations don't just disappear in the middle of the night. Not unless the whole town is haunted or something.

I take one last look around my new room. I guess I'll never find out what that ceiling tastes like. I pull my heavy suitcase toward the door. But all of a sudden I stop. Because I notice a glow coming from outside my window. I notice a *tap tap tap* coming from outside my window.

It's coming from Hopper's house.

I drop my suitcase and rush over to my window. And I stare out at something incredible, something amazing—something very, very, extra-very shocking.

I stare out the window at myself.

Ten

Hopper

The batteries in my flashlight go dead.

The cord on my lamp doesn't stretch far enough.

But then the moon comes out from behind a cloud and throws silver light right where I need it—onto the drawing I put in my window.

The drawing is a sketch of Quinny. I drew it with my charcoal pencils. It wasn't hard, because her face is impossible to forget. It didn't take long, because I didn't draw all twenty-two of her teeth, just the ones you can see in front.

I tap on my window. *Tap tap tap.*

Then again—*tap tap tap.*

I hide behind my window shade.

Quinny comes to her window. She sees the drawing. She looks confused.

But then she smiles.

Okay. Now I can go back to bed. It is much easier to fall asleep when you feel good.

Tomorrow, maybe I'll teach Quinny how to juggle.

Eleven

Quinny

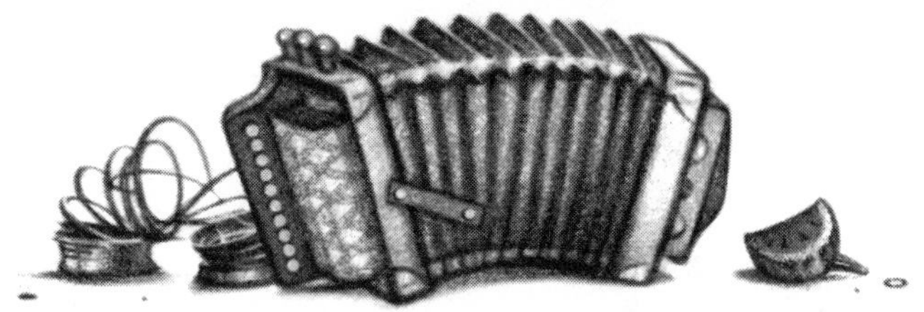

I didn't know Hopper could draw so great. I didn't know he remembered my face so much. And I had no idea my teeth were so beautiful!

It takes me a long time to finish staring at myself. Finally I get back into bed, but it's hard to stay there, so I get up and look at my picture some more.

Then I figure out why I can't sleep. My picture is all by itself. It has nobody to talk to. I think it might be lonely.

I have no idea where all my art stuff is, but I find an empty moving box—#29. *Rip!*

I tiptoe to the bathroom and unzip Mom's

makeup bag. She's got all kinds of pencils and crayons in here. It would be rude to wake her up, so I borrow just a few.

Back in my room, I draw a crinkly forehead and a careful, quiet mouth and a pair of looking-looking eyes. My picture is a little crooked. I guess my fingers can't draw as fancy

as Hopper's, but so what? His mouth can't talk as much as mine.

I lean my cardboard picture of Hopper against my window, facing out at his paper picture of me.

There.

Now these two can keep each other company while Hopper and I sleep.

Twelve

Hopper

Teaching a person how to juggle isn't easy. Especially if that person is Quinny.

I'm too shy to knock on her door, so Mom calls her house after breakfast. Thirty seconds later, Quinny is standing right in front of me. Smiling. She's not even out of breath. She's got a watermelon barrette in her hair, but she smells like peaches.

"Hi, Hopper!" she cries. "Guess what! That chicken named Freya came clucking at our door again, but she ran off before I could talk to her. Plus then, in my cup of milk at breakfast I had the biggest bubble ever!"

I don't know what to say to that, so I turn

and walk upstairs. Quinny follows me. I go into my room. She keeps following me.

Quinny stares at my fish tank full of clown fish and crabs. She stares at my foot model full of bones. She stares at my eyeball, brain, and heart, all lined up on the shelf next to my foot.

"Wow, Hopper, your brothers were right. You've got tons of body parts in here!"

"I'm saving up for a whole skeleton."

"A real one?"

"No, a plastic one. Like the kind they use to train doctors in medical school."

Then Quinny notices my favorite book, *Atlas of Human Anatomy* by Frank H. Netter. She picks it up. "Wow, it's so heavy! What's inside this thing?"

"Please be careful with that." I help her be careful. The book is special.

We open it. We turn the pages gently.

I show Quinny what the inside of a person's head looks like. "That's very, very, extra-very beautiful," she says. "And kind of weird."

"This is where you feel sad." I point to the

limbic system, deep inside the brain. "And also where you feel happy."

"Well, I get sad in my stomach," says Quinny. "I get happy in my nose."

And in her teeth, too, I think.

"So where is it?" she asks.

I don't understand this question.

"My picture. You know, the one you drew of my face last night? With the skin on?"

Oh that. I took it out of my window this morning and slid it under my bed so Trevor and Ty wouldn't see it when they left for soccer practice. I pull it out. I show it to Quinny.

"I look so quiet," she says.

"I made up that part."

"You're good at drawing teeth," she says.

"Thanks. You're good at having teeth."

What I mean is, I like Quinny's smile—but you can't just say that, especially not to a girl. My face feels hot. I decide to change the subject.

I pull out my beanbags and toss them up into a basic three-ball cascade.

"Wow, Hopper, you're the best juggler in the world!"

I switch over into a cross-arm reverse cascade. Quinny gasps and laughs and grabs one of the beanbags from the air as I juggle. "Can I try?" she cries.

"Of course. But not with these." I put down the beanbags and pull out two thin blue silk scarves instead.

"Scarves?"

"Silk juggling scarves. They're lightweight, so they float in the air and are easier for beginners to catch."

"Sounds boring. How about juggling knives?"

"Quinny, just give it a try."

"Or fire sticks! I think the best way to learn juggling is with fire sticks! Because then you would really pay attention!"

I hand Quinny the scarves. I teach her how to juggle. I teach her and teach her. But she doesn't exactly learn. She ties one of the juggling scarves around her head like a pirate, and the other one around her body like a genie.

"Quinny, pay attention."

"I'm starving," she says. "Let's get a snack!"

We go downstairs to the kitchen, and I fix us some cheese and crackers. Quinny points to a photo album lying open on the counter and cries, "Hey! Look, there she is! Freya the chicken!"

She's looking at an old photo from my mom's birthday party last year. I forgot that Freya

came too. “Who’s that old man with her?” Quinny asks.

“That’s Mr. McSoren. He used to live next door to us.”

“He did? You mean, in *my* house?”

“No, in his house. You weren’t there yet.”

“Well, I can’t believe how happy they look together. That chicken is practically glowing!”

I can tell Quinny wants to hear more about the chicken and Mr. McSoren, but it’s a long story, and, to be honest, I’d rather get back to juggling. We’ve still got a lot of work to do.

“Here, let’s eat.” I slide a plate over to Quinny.

After some cheese and crackers and a lot more practice, Quinny finally learns how to juggle scarves. Sort of. “Hopper, look! I’m juggling! I’m really juggling!”

Her technique is sloppy, but you’ve got to start somewhere.

“Thanks for teaching me how to juggle! Now I’ll teach you something.”

“Like what?”

"Did you know that *shampoo* has the word *poo* in it?"

I stare at Quinny. Everybody knows that.

"What about . . . do you know how to whistle for a taxi?"

I shake my head. Quinny pulls me downstairs and outside, right in front of my house. She sticks her hand into her mouth, like she is biting down on two fingers. She whistles so loud it shocks me into standing up straight. When I try it, all I get is soggy fingers.

Quinny whistles and whistles. The street is empty, as usual.

"Oh well." She shrugs. "It worked in the city."

But then a car finally turns the corner. Only it's not a taxi. It's something worse.

Much, much worse.

"Run!" I grab Quinny's hand and pull her away from the street.

Thirteen

Quinny

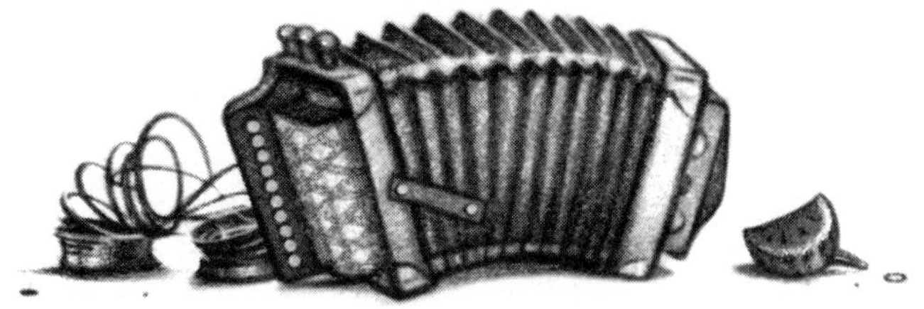

That Hopper is much stronger than he looks! He pulls and pulls me into his backyard, away from the minivan that's turning into his driveway. I look back to see those bully twin brothers of his burst out of the van and run in our direction.

I think they saw us!

Then Hopper lifts a wood flap under his back porch and pulls me through the tiny opening. It's dark in here, but we can see out to the yard through tiny square holes in the wood. It feels safe and cozy to sit in the good-smelly, soft-wormy dirt underneath Hopper's back porch.

"This is fun!"

"Shhh," Hopper shushes me.

We watch the bully twins kick a soccer ball around the backyard. I can't tell which bullyhead is Trevor and which is Ty.

"They're home early," whispers Hopper. "Soccer practice usually goes till noon."

"Hopper, am I a secret?"

"Shhh," he shushes me again, which I guess answers my question.

Trevor (or Ty?) keeps kicking that soccer ball around, while Ty (or Trevor?) pulls a giant soccer net out from behind the garage. Then they start kicking the ball into that net. There's no way Hopper and I can get out of here without them seeing us. Hopper seems too scared to try, even though I've got some tae kwon do moves that could for sure flatten those bully twins.

"Why are they so mean?" I ask him.

"I said shhh."

"They're bullies."

"They're my brothers."

"They hurt you."

"They don't realize it. I know how to stay out of their way."

"Big brothers are supposed to be nice and protect their little brothers," I inform him.

"Is that how it works in your family?"

Hopper has a good point. At least I've never swung Piper around by her ankles.

Trevor and Ty keep kicking the soccer ball into the net. Over and over and over.

"Hopper, I think your brothers are soccer maniacs."

"My parents are, too. They played soccer when they were in school. We go to all my brothers' games. I spend all weekend in the car sometimes because they're on a travel team."

"Wow, that really stinks."

"It's not that bad. I bring stuff to do. I read or draw. And the games are sometimes interesting to watch. Until all the grown-ups start yelling, at least."

I love it here under the porch, in the dirt, in the dark. I love the way the ground smells deep and mushroomy, and the way Hopper is talking to me so much about his life.

And then, all of a sudden, I love the way I am getting SOAKED!

Because it starts raining under the porch, and I hear the *boom-boom* thunder of footsteps above us and Trevor and Ty laughing like they just did something sneaky-horrible-brilliant, except they don't realize they just did me a favor because I love getting soaked!

But, uh-oh—not everyone does.

"BOCK BOCK BOCK!"

I feel wet, tickly-sneezy feathers flap-flap-flapping and rough, pokey claw-feet scratching and splashing mud all over me, and I roll onto Hopper, who's wet and muddy, too, and we crawl around the muck under the porch and the rain keeps coming down hard and I am laughing until I can't get air and Hopper finally pulls me out from the goopy-sloopy dark of the biggest mud puddle ever and into the sunshine and—guess what! A chicken hops out, too!

It's that killer zebra-chicken named Freya! She's muddy and she's mad.

Freya sees the bully twins standing on the porch holding a water hose.

"BOCKBOCKBOCKBOCKBOCKBOCK!!"

They drop the hose and run away. Ha! Those bully twins are chicken of a chicken!

Freya chases them around the yard and flaps her stylish killer feathers and pecks at their ankles with her powerful beak. *"BOCK BOCK BOCK!"* she bocks. *"BOCK BOCK BOCK!"*

"Go, Freya, go!" I jump and clap and cheer for that gutsy bird.

Then I notice the water hose just lying there. So I pick it up and hand it to Hopper and point over at the bully twins, who are still running away from Freya like chickens with their heads cut off. "Hopper, what are you waiting for? Now's your chance to get those bullies back!"

Hopper looks at me like I'm crazy, but I press that hose into his hand and push him forward.

"Go for it!"

Fourteen

Hopper

I'm not brave enough to do this.

But Quinny thinks I am, and just in case she's right, I aim the hose at my brothers and press the handle. Water bursts out, fast and freezing cold.

"Aaaaahhhh!" Trevor yelps as I soak him in the stomach.

"Grrrrrrrr!" Ty roars as I spray him in the nose.

"Wait, wait, wait!" cries Quinny.

She leans over and changes the setting on the hose sprayer from *stream* to *jet*. The water blasts out faster now. Trevor and Ty scream louder.

Quinny puts her hand over mine on the hose. We press that handle down, hard.

I'm dead meat, for sure.

But I think it might be worth it.

Fifteen

Quinny

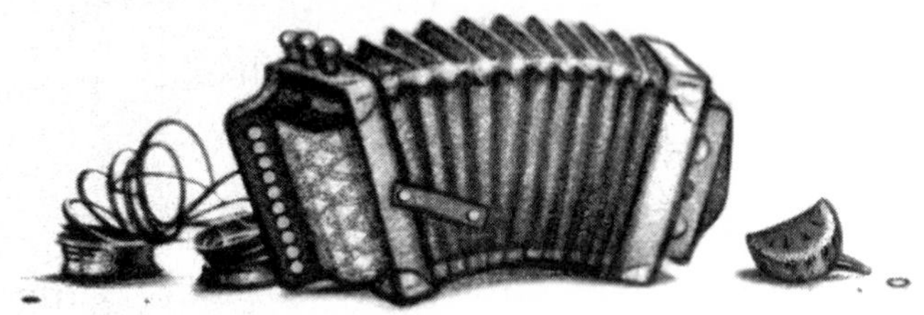

How was I supposed to know that Mrs. Porridge would pick this exact moment to walk into Hopper's yard?

And that she would come by with her cat on a leash?

And that both she and that cat—who is so huge it looks more like a bear cub—hate being accidentally sprayed with freezing water from a garden hose?

"Reeeeeeeee!" screeches that soaked cat.

"Good heavens," cries that soaked old lady.

"BOCK BOCK BOCK!" bocks muddy Freya, who suddenly wants a piece of that cat.

"Hiiiisssssssssss!" hisses the cat, trying to sink its fangs into Freya's feathers.

Mrs. Porridge kicks that killer chicken away from her chubby cat, but they all get tangled up in the cat's leash. "Leave my Walter alone, you birdbrained terrorist!"

"Good morning, Mrs. Porridge!" I call out. "How are you? This must be your cat, who you just called Walter, so I think he's probably a boy cat, right? But how did he get so huge? And why are you walking him on a leash? Is he part dog?"

"My dress!" cries a soaked girl, who was walking with Mrs. Porridge and Walter, except I didn't even see that girl until now. Because if a gigantic, wet cat starts fighting a muddy killer chicken, that's usually the first thing people notice.

"Wow, Mrs. Porridge, I didn't know you have a girl, too!"

"This is my grand-niece, Victoria," huffs Mrs. Porridge. "She's visiting for the day, and I was under the mistaken impression that you two might like to meet each other."

I look at Victoria again. She's wearing a very glamorous, very complicated itchy-pink dress. A very soggy itchy-pink dress. Her sparkly headband and stylish purse and high-heely sandals are also itchy-pink and wet-ish. She looks like the kind of beautiful, expensive doll you are not allowed to touch, except that someone dropped that doll into a puddle.

Before I can ask Victoria if she was on her way to a party, she sputters, "This dress is *dry clean only*!"

Uh-oh.

Dry clean only = you have to take it to a special store + pay a lot of money to have it cleaned with chemicals that are not good for our planet, according to Mom. But Daddy used to dry-clean-only all his work shirts back in New York City, which is how I know so much about it.

I also know we owe Victoria an apology. Hopper looks too scared to say it, so I do.

"Sorry, Victoria. Hey, too bad that dress isn't wet clean only."

Victoria glares at us.

"Dry clean? Wet clean? Get it? By the way, I'm Quinny and this is Hopper."

Victoria stomps off wetly without even laughing at my joke. Mrs. Porridge picks up her giant, drippy cat and follows in her grand-niece's foot stomps.

"Quinny, what on earth is going on?" says Mom, who must have shown up while I wasn't looking and does not seem too happy.

Then I notice Piper, too, peeking out from behind a tree, all half naked and sneaky-smiley. "Quinny didded it!" she blurts out. "She soaked that old lady and her cat and her pretty girl!"

"*Didded* is not a word," I inform my grimy little sister. "And put a shirt on, you chimpanzee."

Now that we live in the middle of nowhere, Piper has stopped wearing clothes. She likes to go outside in her underpants or a swimsuit bottom and roll around in the grass like some wild animal. She won't even come inside to pee—she just squats behind this one tree in our yard, like a dog. Daddy calls that spot her "invisible toilet"—you won't catch me going anywhere near it.

"I sawed the whole thing," Piper tattles. "It was Quinny."

"Tattletale for sale!" I call out. "Tattletale for sale!"

"All right, Quinny, that's enough trouble for one day," says Mom. "In the house, now."

"But it's not even lunchtime!"

Mom drags me home anyway. I look back at Hopper, who's getting dragged off by his own mad mom, along with the bully twins, whose two mouths are blaming the whole thing on Hopper, which is a lie, but I can't even defend him, because Mom shuts our door and orders me upstairs and makes me take a whole entire bath, even though I just took one two days ago.

Piper tries to jump in the tub, too, because we sometimes still take our baths together, but I don't want that snoopy wild animal anywhere near me right now. "Get your germy butt out of here!" I screech at her, making my best ferocious face.

Mom plucks chicken feathers from my hair and scrubs my muddy face and mutters, "How on earth, Quinny? How on earth?"

After my bath, she makes me write a letter saying sorry to Mrs. Porridge and offering to pay to dry-clean-only Victoria's dress from my allowance. Which isn't fair, because Trevor and Ty started it with the water hose. Just like they started it with the broken vase yesterday. Why oh why did we have to move next door to such beastly bully twins? I don't even want to think about what those monsters are doing to Hopper right now. I just hope he's still alive.

I sit there, sinking to the very bottom of this very bad mood, when I feel a licky-wet finger slime my ankle. It's Piper again, under the table. She almost gets away, but I grab that nosy little beast by the tail—I mean ponytail—and pull her back to me, ever so gently.

"Hello, tattletale." I squish her cheeks between my knees. "This is not your lucky day."

Sixteen

Hopper

Because of all the trouble with the water hose, Mom sends us to our rooms to "spend some quiet time thinking about how to make better choices."

I know I should have said sorry to Victoria and Mrs. Porridge for accidentally soaking them. But Victoria makes me nervous. She never says hi to me, even though we were in the same second-grade class last year. She acts like it costs her money to be nice to people, and she doesn't think I'm worth it.

Being sent to my room is usually my favorite punishment. But this time Trevor pounds on the wall between his room and mine. "Dead meat! Dead meat! Dead meat!" Ty plays his brain-exploding video game really loud. I wonder how my brothers will get me back for getting them back with that water hose. I'm sure they are wondering the same thing.

At dinnertime, I pretend I have a stomachache so I can stay in my room.

At bedtime, I pretend I'm already asleep so I can keep staying in my room.

Mom brings me plain toast and touches my forehead to see if I have a fever. Dad pulls the covers up to my chin. After my parents leave, I get up and drag my chair over to block my door. Just in case Trevor and Ty get any crazy ideas in the middle of the night.

When I wake up in the morning, luckily I am still alive. And my brothers have to leave for soccer camp before they can do anything too horrible to get me back.

"You're still dead meat," says Trevor as he punches my arm good-bye.

"You and that crazy chicken," says Ty as he slaps the side of my head. "We're gonna eat that thing for dinner when we get back."

Dad helps them pack their duffel bags into the minivan. They're taking a lot of stuff because they'll be living at soccer camp for the rest of the summer. That's fine with me. Now the house will feel calmer. My body will feel safer.

As Trevor and Ty ride away, Quinny waves out at them from her bedroom window and sticks her tongue out. "Bock bock bock!" she screams.

After the minivan turns the corner, she runs outside and into my yard and over to my brothers' soccer net. She tips the whole thing over.

"What are you doing?" I catch up to her.

"Trespassing!" She smiles.

The soccer net falls forward onto its metal frame with a thump.

"If you break that thing, they're going to kill you," I tell her.

Quinny climbs onto the sideways net and lies on it, like it's a hammock.

I stare up at her staring up at the sky.

"What are you waiting for?" she says. "Get up here!"

I think about it. I shake my head.

"Come on, Hopper! It's fun."

I look around. My brothers are gone. I get up there. I lie there next to Quinny. We swing a little in the warm breeze. My body feels lighter now. Like I'm floating on my back at the town pool.

"See?" Quinny smiles.

I look up and I see. The sky is blue, with one small cloud in the shape of a hippocampus. That's the part of your brain where you remember your life.

Seventeen

Quinny

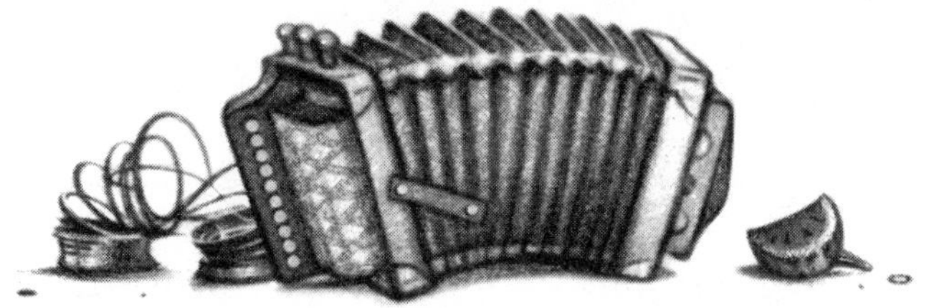

This is my luckiest summer ever.

The bully twins just left for sleepaway camp, plus Piper went to the pediatrician because she has an itchy rash on her bottom. (She picked up booty cooties from peeing outside, I think.) So it's just me and Hopper, hanging out in the clever hammock that I invented from the bully twins' useless soccer net, and we have the whole day to do whatever we want.

Except I think I feel my body falling.

Crack! Plop! I'm suddenly splat on the ground, with grass up my nose and Hopper's arms and legs all twisted up in mine. I look around. The metal frame of this soccer-net hammock has cracked into two chunks.

Hopper looks terrified. "This thing was brand-new."

"Well, if I were your brothers, I'd ask for my money back."

Hopper is breathing funny now. His eyes bulge out. I can tell he is picturing himself being swung around upside down by his ankles, faster and faster until he barfs.

"Don't worry, Hopper. Those bully twins are far away at soccer camp for, like, a million weeks, and I don't think your mom even saw—plus I know just how to fix this thing. Wait here!"

I run over to my house. I find a tape gun—which I'm not allowed to touch, because it has sharp parts, but we've got a bunch left over from moving, and I'm more responsible than my parents think, so I don't see what the big deal is if I borrow this tape gun for just two seconds.

I run back out to Hopper's yard. I use the tape gun to wrap sticky brownish moving-box tape around the two broken metal pieces of the soccer-net frame.

SCREEEEECH SCREEEECH SCREEEECH, yells the tape gun.

There. Good as new. Sort of.

"Quinny, what are you doing?" Hopper is sitting with his head between his knees now, like how the nurse at school makes you sit when you're barfy sick.

I drag that slightly crooked, taped-up soccer-net-hammock thing back behind Hopper's garage. "We'll just leave it alone to heal," I tell him.

"Heal? That's a broken soccer net, not a broken leg."

"Shhh, it needs to rest. Let's go play." I pull Hopper up and over toward my house.

"But—"

"Come on!"

It's time this boy and I really got to know each other.

I pull him into our kitchen and tell him to close his eyes.

"Why?" he asks.

"Just do it, and no peeking. You'll find out."

I open our refrigerator and pull out some mustard and show it to Hopper's nose.

"Guess what this is. Just from sniffing. And remember, no peeking!"

Hopper sniffs. Then he sniffs again. "Mustard," he guesses.

"Correct!"

He also guesses orange juice and leftover spaghetti correctly. When it's my turn, I guess ketchup and pickles correctly, but then I miss on cream cheese, which is a really hard one.

"Hopper, you won the smelling bee! Congratulations."

Then we go up to the second floor, and I wrap a towel around my head, like a fortune-teller, and I grab my New York City snow globe out of a moving box, and I sit crisscross-applesauce across from Hopper on the floor. I stare into the snow globe, which is almost like a crystal ball. "You will meet a fabulous individual whose name rhymes with *skinny*," I inform him. "You will have your luckiest summer ever with this splendid individual."

Then I show Hopper my room. And what his room looks like from my window.

We figure out that my room's ceiling, which looks like coconut frosting, doesn't taste like coconut frosting. It tastes like needles. Ouch!

I show Hopper my accordion, which I share with Mom, but really it's mostly mine. I offer to play him a song, but his face looks like it's not quite ready for that.

I show him my tae kwon do certificate, which is framed with the piece of wood that I broke in half with my strong, kicky, bare foot to earn my green belt.

Then Hopper notices my bulletin board, full of photos from school and theater camp and tae kwon do and playdates and birthday parties and sleepovers and Central Park adventures.

He stares at this big photo collage. "Who are all those people?" he asks.

"Those are my friends from the city."

"All of them?"

"No, not all of them, silly. I didn't have enough room on there for *all* my friends. But now that we live here, I've got more wall space, so I can get another bulletin board and make a second photo collage and add even more friends! Hey, want to help me do that now?"

Hopper looks down and mumbles, "No, thanks."

"But I noticed you're so great at art stuff, maybe we could—"

"Bock bock," says Hopper.

Except it's not really Hopper saying it—it's that stylish killer zebra-chicken, Freya! I look outside and see her clucking her brains out again, right at my kitchen door.

I rush downstairs. *"BOCK!"* Freya glares at me through the window in the door. Her beady little eyes look confused and her crabby clucks sound full of angry hurt. Before I can open the door to ask her what's wrong, she runs away. Again.

"What's the story with that chicken?" I ask Hopper. "She keeps coming here and looking inside my house, like she wants to be friends. But then she runs away."

"That chicken does not want to be your friend. She only likes Mr. McSoren."

"Where's Mr. McSoren now?" I ask.

"I don't know. One day an ambulance came and took him away."

"Oh no! What happened?"

"My parents said he fell down the stairs," says Hopper. "And the chicken got out somehow. People in the neighborhood tried to catch it. But it was no use. Freya's too fast. And she's mean to everyone except Mr. McSoren."

I don't think that chicken is mean in a mean way. I think that chicken is mean in a lonely way. There's a difference. "Poor chicken. No wonder she comes clucking at our back door—she must be so confused and upset. Why didn't Mr. McSoren ever come back for her?"

"Maybe he gotted dead," says Pee-U Piper.

I didn't realize my little sister was back from the pediatrician. "Stop snooping and go scratch your itchy butt," I growl at her, then turn back to Hopper. "It's not true, is it, Hopper? Please say Freya's roommate isn't dead!"

"Mr. McSoren was pretty old," says Hopper. "But I'm not really sure."

"Well, he can't be dead, because then what'll happen to that poor homeless chicken? Who's going to feed her and take care of her, and what about winter, when it gets really cold—"

"Quinny, breathe."

"She lost her home and her best friend—we've got to find him! Where on earth did Mr. McSoren go?"

"I don't know," says Hopper with a sigh. "But I know someone who might."

Eighteen

Hopper

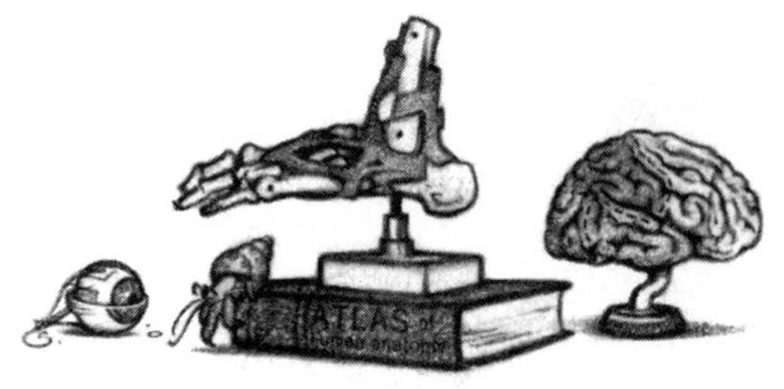

Who cares about a chicken?

Quinny cares. I have no idea why, but she does.

And that makes me care. I have no idea why, but I do. So I lead Quinny down the street. When she realizes whose house we're going to, she freaks out again.

"But Mrs. Porridge hates us because we soaked her chubby cat, Walter, plus her grand-niece, Victoria, with that freezing water hose!"

"I'm sure they've all dried off by now. Do you want some answers or not?"

I lead Quinny up to Mrs. Porridge's front door and knock. Nobody answers, so we go around back and find Mrs. Porridge in her garden, yanking weeds. She's got Walter tied to her fence with his cat leash. He looks about as unhappy as she does.

"What now?" snaps Mrs. Porridge.

We explain what, but she is not interested in helping us help Freya.

"Oh, pish, you won't see me going anywhere near that crazy old bird," says Mrs. Porridge. "I

tried to catch it once, and all I got for my trouble was a bunch of peck marks! Bottom line is, that chicken won't tolerate anyone but Herbert McSoren."

"But where did Mr. McSoren go?" I ask.

"What do I look like, a private detective?" says Mrs. Porridge. "If he wanted that squawky bag of feathers, he'd have come back for it. Or maybe the old geezer finally croaked."

"Don't say that!" wails Quinny.

"If you children will excuse me, I don't have time to waste on things that are a waste of time."

"But we've got to help her, somehow!" Quinny cries. "She's so upset and confused. She comes clucking at our back door every day."

"Don't worry. Pretty soon a possum or a hawk will snatch that chicken up, and you'll get some peace and quiet."

"No!"

"Come on." I pull Quinny away. "I have another idea."

We walk back to my house. I make a phone call. To a number I know by heart.

"No, he's not dead," Grandpa Gooley says to me on the phone. "Herbert McSoren is living up in Milford with his sister now."

Quinny pulls at the phone so she can hear, too. She squeals and hops up and down at this good news. Her hair tickles my cheek, but it's the good kind of tickle.

"He can't get around too well since he took that fall down the stairs," Grandpa Gooley says. "I know his sister's been back here a couple of times trying to catch that chicken, but it won't go near anybody but him."

"That's what Mrs. Porridge said!" cries Quinny. "But there's got to be a way!"

"It's a miracle Freya's still alive, what with all the foxes out there," he says.

"Please oh please won't you help us, Grandpa Gooley?" Quinny begs. "Pleeeease?"

"He's not your grandpa," I point out.

"Well, I'd be happy to give you a ride up there," Grandpa Gooley says, chuckling. "But you've got to catch that chicken first."

Nineteen

Quinny

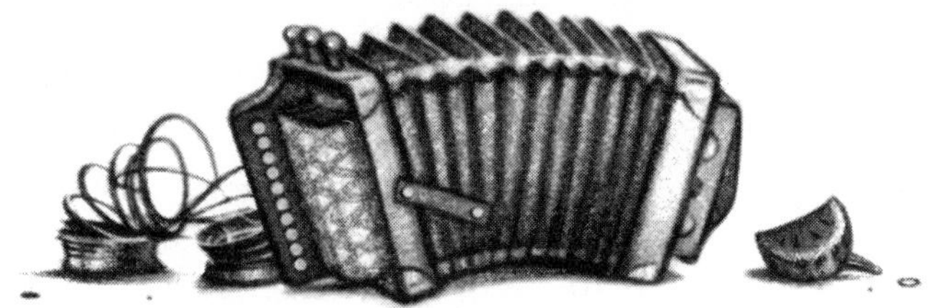

How on earth am I going to catch a chicken?

I put on my sneakers. I do some stretches to warm up.

But chasing her doesn't work. Freya's too fast.

So I try sitting still. I fill a bowl with dried corn and sit very calm and gentle outside my kitchen door. I hold out the bowl and cluck as chickenly as possible.

"Bock bock bock," I bock sweetly. "Bock bock bock."

Hopper opens his bedroom window and looks out at me. "Freya doesn't know she's a chicken," he says. “Mr. McSoren always talked to her like a regular person.”

“Dear Freya!” I call out. “You are the most stylish, most beautiful zebra-chicken-person in the world! You are special, you are spiffy, you are fan-fluffy-tastic!”

That doesn’t work, either.

“Maybe not so loud,” says Hopper.

Mrs. Porridge walks by with Walter on his leash. “Goodness gracious, we could hear you hollering all the way up the street,” she grumps. Then she sees what I’m holding. “You’ll have to do better than plain old corn. That persnickety chicken likes worms and freshly killed grasshoppers.”

My insides shiver. Freshly killed *what*?

“Freya eats from our songbird feeder, too,” says Hopper. “And once I saw Mr. McSoren feed her potato chips right out of his hand.”

Potato chips? We’ve got a big bag of those in the kitchen! So I make a trail of chips starting at the bird feeder in Hopper’s yard and leading over to my house and into my kitchen. But squirrels and birds gobble those chips up before Freya even notices them.

I keep trying.

I make a trail of Cheerios, mushy grapes, and string cheese. I set out stale marshmallows and leftover spaghetti and croutons. Broccoli, tortilla chips, and a big, stinky red onion, too. Piper even hands over a few icky, half-rotted wormy bits from her collection of backyard gunk.

Every morning, I put food out.

Every morning, Freya keeps coming by to peck at it. But she won't come into the kitchen and she always runs off before I can get close enough to grab her.

So I make a lasso out of an old jump rope. I practice lassoing on Hopper.

It turns out he's much easier to catch than Freya.

Still, I don't give up. I'm going to catch that chicken if it takes me all summer.

Grandpa Gooley comes to visit Hopper one morning in the middle of August. "Freya can sense you coming from a mile away," he tells me. "You've got to sneak up on her." He gives me a big net on a stick from his car. "Technically, it's for catching fish. But I'll bet it works on chickens, too."

"Thanks, Grandpa Gooley!" I swing that net through the air. I pretend I'm sneaking up on a chicken. This could work!

But what's sneakier than sneaking up on someone? Sneaking *down* on them, of course. So I build a pile of gummy worms (the next best thing to real worms) in Hopper's bird feeder. Then I climb the big tree next to it and sit on a long, thick branch. Now I'm high enough over that bird feeder so Freya won't see me, but low enough to reach down and scoop her into the net.

"What makes you think chickens don't look up?" Hopper asks from down on the ground.

"Shhh," I tell him. "Get up here."

Hopper climbs the tree and keeps me company as I wait. It's fun, at first. We can see my whole yard from up here. His, too. But we can't talk or we'll scare away Freya. Pretty soon my bottom gets sore from sitting on this pokey tree branch. And my mouth gets twitchy from not talking. And my stomach grumbles of boredom.

"Shhh," I tell my stomach.

Just when I think I can't wait in this tree a minute longer, Freya finally shows up. She looks around, all careful and suspicious, and then hops up onto the bird feeder and starts pecking away at those gummy worms.

This is it! I reach down to catch her with the net. But I'm so excited that I guess I reach a little too far. My balance wobbles and my grip slips, and no, no, no—I get that quick-sicky roller-coaster feeling in my tummy as I tumble off that tree branch.

I'm falling . . . I'm falling right onto Freya!

Twenty

Hopper

I catch Quinny by her ankle. She dangles upside down off the tree branch, swinging the net around like crazy while Freya clucks at her head and then runs away.

"Let go of me!" Quinny shouts. "I almost caught her!"

"You almost crushed your skull," I tell her.

Both of our moms come outside to see what all the noise is about. They help Quinny get right side up again.

"Quinny, please! Your head is more important than a chicken," says her mom. "I hate to think what would have happened if Hopper hadn't been here."

"I would've caught that chicken, that's what would've happened."

"Quinny!"

"But I was so close!"

"What do we say to Hopper?"

"Thank you for saving my head's life," she mutters.

"Nice try, Quinny." My mom chuckles. "Too bad we can't just hypnotize that chicken."

"What?"

Then my mom explains how Mr. McSoren used to hypnotize Freya all the time. "It was amazing the way he could control her."

Quinny looks at me all excited now. "Hopper, why didn't you tell me that? I'll hypnotize Freya, too! Then she'll do whatever I want!"

"It's not that simple," I warn her.

"That's okay. I'll practice on you first so I can get really good," she says. "Hold still, pretend you're a chicken, and look into my eyes."

"Quinny—"

"You are getting sleepy."

"That's not—"

"You are getting very, very, extra-very sleepy—"

"No, I'm not. I'm wide awake and standing here talking to you."

Quinny takes a good look at me. She realizes that I'm right. "Great," she sighs. "If I can't even hypnotize a boy, how will I ever hypnotize a chicken?"

"How about some ice cream?" I suggest, changing the subject.

"Great idea! I'm starving!"

Quinny's always starving. She follows me into my kitchen. I scoop chocolate ice cream onto two plain cones. Quinny crunches into her cone before I even finish licking the top of mine.

"Quinny, if you ever catch Freya—"

"You mean *when we* catch Freya," she corrects me. "We're a team, remember?"

A team.

I can't believe Quinny said that. Maybe it's even true.

"Fine . . . *when we* catch Freya," I say, "how

are we going to keep her caught long enough to bring her to Mr. McSoren?"

"I don't know. She's pretty wiggly," she says. "That's a good question."

Then I take Quinny down to my basement and show her a good answer.

Twenty-one

Quinny

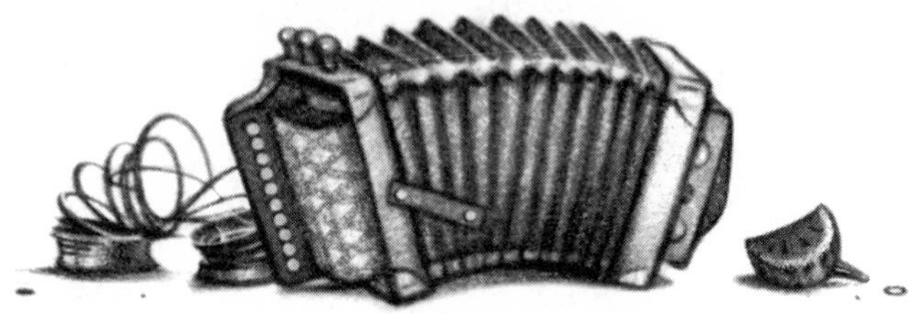

In a dark, dusty corner of his basement, Hopper shows me a big metal cage called a dog crate. He tells me his family once had a dog named Score that slept in this crate in their kitchen, but then the dog died when Hopper was just a toddler, so they didn't need the crate anymore.

"That's so sad," I tell Hopper. "I'm sorry about your poor dead dog."

"He was really old. I don't even remember him."

I can't imagine not remembering the first dog I ever had. "Well, I've been wanting an alive dog for ages now," I say. "But my parents keep bringing home little sisters instead."

Then I notice that this dog crate has a door that locks with a latch. And it looks like it would fit in the backseat of a car.

The good news is, Freya can ride in this crate all the way to Mr. McSoren's new house!

The grumpy news is, we've still got to get Freya inside the crate.

Early the next morning, Hopper and I drag that crate upstairs and over to my yard. We push it right up against my kitchen door, which is still Freya's favorite clucking spot. We stick tons of scrumptious food inside: a watermelon lollipop and a plate of crispy orange cheese doodles, which look kind of like worms, if you ask me, plus a bunch of barbecue potato chips, because we haven't tried that flavor yet. Then I make Piper sprinkle a few boogers from her nose onto the whole pile of treats. Because you never know what a chicken will eat, and I'm getting kind of desperate here.

Then Hopper ties some rope to the crate's open door. We hide behind a nearby bush and hold that rope.

And then we wait.

The plan is, when Freya steps into the crate to peck at all those booger-flavored treats, we'll pull the rope to shut the door, and—*poof*—we'll have ourselves one caught chicken!

After waiting a long time behind that bush, we keep waiting. It turns out that sitting quietly behind a bush is even more boring than sitting quietly up in a tree.

"What if Freya doesn't like boogers?" I whisper to Hopper.

"Shhh, here she comes."

It's about time. Freya chicken-hops over to the crate. She *bock-bock*s at it, like it has no right being there by *her* kitchen door.

"Bock bock BOCK!"

Then Freya sees the cheese doodles inside the crate. She sees those intriguing barbecue-booger potato chips.

"Bockbockbockbockbockbockbock!"

But instead of hopping into the crate to gobble up everything, that chicken squeezes her skinny, stretchy head through the bars, and her sneaky little beak reaches all the food no problem.

"Hey, no fair!" I yell at that cheating chicken.

Freya turns and glares over at us behind the bush. *"Booooooooooooock!"*

(I'm pretty sure that means "Nice try, stupid humans" in chicken-talk.)

And then she runs off with the watermelon lollipop in her beak.

Hopper laughs. Which is the first time I have ever seen that boy laugh.

But it's not funny. We're back to where we started.

"Any more bright ideas?" I ask him.

"I guess we need a new plan," he says.

"Before Freya gets eaten by a fox," I add. "We're running out of time."

Then I hear Mom start to play the accordion, from inside my house. Which means she's trying to get Cleo to go down for her nap again. She's playing "Yellow Submarine" by the Beatles, one of my favorite songs.

Then Hopper touches my arm and points

across my yard, to below Cleo's window, where something very, very, extra-very amazing is happening.

It's Freya. She's standing there, listening to Mom play.

I creep over to that chicken. Slowly. But the music stops before I get there.

"Booooooooock!" Freya clucks, and runs away again.

"Hopper! Did you see that? Freya loves music!"

"Mr. McSoren used to play the harmonica."

"He did? Well, did you know that I play the accordion, too?"

"I think the whole neighborhood knows that."

"An accordion sounds just like a giant harmonica! I bet Freya will come closer if I play! She'll be so amazed by my amazing accordion that she'll follow me right into the kitchen!"

"Maybe," says Hopper. I can tell he really means *maybe not*.

But I try to think positive because then maybe positive will come true.

"So what songs did Mr. McSoren play?"

"I don't know. A whole bunch."

"Like what? Tell me!"

"He played 'Home on the Range' sometimes . . . and 'On Top of Old Smokey.'"

"Did he ever play any songs by the Beatles? Because I know a ton of those!"

"I don't think so," says Hopper. "But I remember, on the Fourth of July he would always play 'Yankee Doodle Dandy,' and Freya would cluck and dance around to it."

Hey, I actually kind of almost know that song! Part of it, at least. I run inside. I find my big book of accordion sheet music. I flip and flip the pages until I find it—"Yankee Doodle Dandy." I go over all the notes.

Then I get my accordion from Mom and slide it on and stand in the kitchen by the open door to our yard. Hopper grabs the net and hides behind the door, ready to catch Freya once she steps inside.

Then I play "Yankee Doodle Dandy." And I even get most of the notes right.

Then I play it again. And again.

I look over at Hopper. He peeks outside and shrugs. No Freya.

I play it again. And again. And again and again.

But I guess that chicken is not very patriotic after all.

Finally I slip the accordion off and slump down to the floor. My arms hurt. My engine is out of gas. "I give up," I tell Hopper. "Freya's doomed."

Twenty-two

Hopper

I look down at Quinny frowning on the floor. "We can't give up now," I tell her.

"Easy for you to say. You're not the one whose arms are falling off from playing 'Yankee Doodle Dandy' a gazillion times."

"But, Quinny, look." I point outside.

Freya's peeking out from some bushes at the back of the yard. She seems confused.

"She's listening!" cries Quinny. "She wonders why the music stopped!"

Quinny slides the accordion back onto her chest and starts playing again. Freya hops closer to the house. I hide behind the kitchen door again. I'll push it closed right after she hops inside and then I'll scoop her into the net.

Freya hops closer and closer. She's only a few feet away now.

Today is the day we'll catch her. I can feel it.

Quinny feels it, too. I can tell. She smiles as she plays her accordion louder and faster. The beat of her music thumps inside my chest. Being with Quinny feels like being by myself, only better. We're a team.

I wish this summer would never end.

Freya's at the door now. She's getting ready to hop inside. Quinny keeps playing. I keep gripping the net. This is it. We're about to catch that chicken.

But then, we don't.

Just as Freya steps into the kitchen, Quinny's little sister runs in, wearing only her underpants and waving an envelope. "Snail mail!" she screams. "You gotted snail mail!"

And Freya hops back outside and runs away. *"Bockbockbockbockbock!"*

Just like that, she's gone. My whole body

feels like a flat tire now.

"Piper, how could you!" Quinny cries. "We almost had her!"

"Look, you gotted snail mail! Open it, open it!"

"Go away. You ruined everything!"

Quinny takes the envelope from Piper. It's addressed to *Eleanor Quinston Bumble.*

"Who's that?" I ask.

"It's me," says Quinny. "Eleanor's my real first name."

I didn't know that about Quinny. Then I notice the return address on that envelope: WHISPER VALLEY ELEMENTARY SCHOOL.

And I get a bad feeling in my stomach. Even worse than how it felt to lose Freya.

Quinny rips open the envelope and reads the letter.

Slowly, her teeth start smiling. Her dimples dig deeper into her happy cheeks. I turn away and close my eyes. Because I know what's in that letter.

I wish this summer would never end. But it just did.

Twenty-three

Quinny

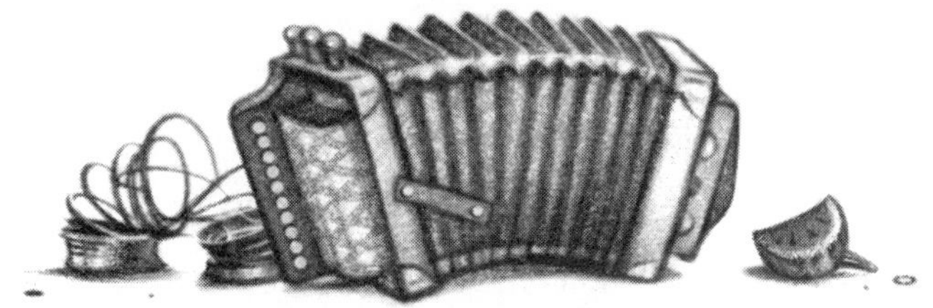

I'm very, very, extra-very mad at Piper for scaring off Freya, but the next-best thing in life to catching a homeless zebra-chicken is getting actual, real-life SNAIL MAIL.

"What does it say? What does it say?" Piper bounces like a little maniac.

"Calm your engine down."

I hold the letter so she can't see, because it's none of her beeswax.

Dear Eleanor Quinston Bumble,

Welcome to the third grade at Whisper Valley Elementary School.

Together we are going to have a wonderful year! My name is Ms. Yoon and I will be your teacher

I stop reading and turn to Hopper. This news is too juicy to keep to myself!

"Hopper, look! School's going to start, and I have Ms. Yoon for third grade. Look, she says it's going to be a wonderful year and—wait, if I got a school letter, maybe you got one, too!"

Hopper just stands there, blinking slowly.

"I bet you got the same letter! Let's check! Let's go check right now."

I grab Hopper's arm, which feels heavier than normal, and pull him over to his house and open up his mailbox, and sure enough, there's an envelope in there from Whisper Valley Elementary School. "Hopper, it came! Look!" I cry. "Open it! Who's your teacher? Who?"

Hopper is being a slowpoke, so I help him open that envelope and, YES, he's in Ms. Yoon's third-grade class, too! This really is my luckiest summer ever!

"Yippeeeee! Hopper, we're going to be in the same class! Starting in just two weeks. How cool is that? You can introduce me to everybody. I'm so excited to meet your friends—hey, should we find out if any of them got Ms. Yoon, too? I bet everyone got their letters today."

Hopper doesn't answer. He looks tired all of a sudden. A little queasy, too. But then I turn over the letter and discover something else that will perk him up for sure.

"Plus look, Hopper! On the back of this letter is a fabulous list of school supplies we need. How convenient! Let's go shopping right now."

"Quinny, please." Mom walks over and rudely interrupts us. "You've had enough excitement for one day."

"Mom, can you drive us to the store? Hopper and I need to get school supplies."

"You need to eat dinner and get ready for bed. Come on."

Instead of going to bed feeling sad that we didn't catch Freya, I go to bed excited about getting that school letter and being together with Hopper in Ms. Yoon's class in just two more weeks. All that excitement rolls down a hill inside me into a bigger and bigger ball of happiness.

The next morning I persuade Daddy to take me shopping for back-to-school supplies.

"Can we ask Hopper to come, too?"

"Quinny, please."

Unfortunately we do have to take Piper and Cleo along because Mom's working. Piper's extra crabby since she has to wear clothes out in public. Cleo's extra gassy since she ate a green bean smoothie for breakfast. I'm squished between the two of them in the backseat as Daddy drives us to a big, giant school-supply supermarket two towns away.

This place has a parking lot and sliding glass doors and shopping carts, just like the grocery store, but instead of apples and cereal and two-percent low-fat milk, the aisles are filled with pencils and notebooks and folders. (The store also has grown-up school supplies, which are called office supplies.)

I get a twelve-pack of pencils plus three folders plus a ruler plus a big thing of glue sticks.

"Quinny, do you want a notebook with flowers on the cover, or hearts?" asks Daddy.

"I'd like a notebook with a chicken on the cover, please."

But they don't have any here. They do have erasers that look like tiny burgers and fries. Those look like they work much better than the basic rectangle kind.

Then I push our cart past a big pile of backpacks. "Hey, I need a new backpack, too!"

"Indoor voice, Quinny," says Daddy.

"Remember how my backpack got ripped last year back in New York when it got stuck in the subway door that time we were running late for school and—"

"How could I forget?"

But the only backpacks in this store are plain blue or plain brown or plain red.

"My favorite color is green with orange polka dots."

"Really? I hadn't heard," Daddy says.

"If we can't find green with orange polka dots, I also love orange with green polka dots."

"That's good to know, Quinny. We'll keep looking."

We turn into the next aisle, and then I see something that is even more exciting than school supplies. It's a big, blank bright-white poster board. Big enough for someone to draw a life-size picture of Mr. McSoren on it . . . which I'm sure Hopper can do since he's an artistic genius. Then we'll put his big drawing of Mr. McSoren right inside my kitchen and leave the door open so Freya sees it, and she'll be so excited to see him again that she'll hop inside, and then we'll sneak up on her with the net and finally—

"Quinny? Hello, earth to Quinny?" Daddy looks down at me. "Let's keep moving."

"Oh, Daddy, I just have to get this poster board! Please? Freya's life depends on it."

Daddy sighs.

We get in line to pay. Piper begs for candy by the cash register. Cleo grabs candy without begging. When Daddy takes it away from her, she cries so hard that the tuba in her diaper plays a fart again. We make a big mess and a big ruckus and a big stink in that store, and people stare big-time.

"This is why you should have left them at home," I tell Daddy as I plug my nose. It's a good thing I didn't run away back to New York City. I'm the only normal, well-behaved child this poor guy's got.

I carry my poster board and my wonderful, swingy bag of school supplies out to the car. On the ride home, Cleo screams and spits up. Piper picks her nose. My sisters are driving me nuts. I can't wait until I get to spend all day every day in Ms. Yoon's beautiful, lovely third-grade classroom with Hopper, who doesn't spit up or share his boogers with the world.

We get home and I'm about to run over to Hopper's house and show him the exciting poster board that we'll use to finally catch Freya, but then I notice a box in the corner of my garage. A big, new box, and it looks like it could be for me.

"What in the world is that?" I ask Daddy.

"Only one way to find out." He winks at me. Which means it *is* for me!

I tear open the box and find a backpack, and it's green with orange polka dots. But wait, there's more: inside the backpack is a matching lunch box, and it's orange with green polka dots.

"My favorite colors! Daddy, how did you know?"

"Wild guess."

I hug Daddy thanks, and I grab my amazing new backpack and that big white poster board, and I run out the garage door and over to Hopper's house.

"Hopper, Hopper, Hopper!" I bang on his front door.

Hopper's dad answers the door.

"Hopper's dad, look what I just got! Plus I need to talk to Hopper."

"That's a snazzy backpack, Quinny," he says. "He's in the kitchen."

I find Hopper sitting at the kitchen table staring at a cauliflower sandwich.

"Hopper, why are you staring at that sandwich? Did you find out if your other friends are in Ms. Yoon's class, too? Plus guess what, I went shopping for school supplies and saw this giant poster board, and I figured out a way for us to catch Freya! Oh, and check it out: here's my exciting new backpack! It's so roomy I can fit all my school supplies in here!"

Hopper looks at the poster board and then at my backpack. He doesn't look too excited. He just shrugs and walks upstairs. So I rush up after him.

But Hopper won't come out of his room. He won't let me into it, either.

I knock. I wait. I knock again. "Hopper, please open the door."

"Go away."

"Come on, let's play. Wait till you hear how we're going to catch Freya! All you have to do is draw a big picture of Mr. McSoren on this poster and then—"

“I don’t care.”

“What?”

“Just leave me alone. I don’t want to play.”

“Why not?”

“Stop it.”

“C’mon Hopper, please?”

“I said go away and leave me alone!”

“But—”

“Are you stupid? Don’t you get it? It’s over!”

Hopper booms this very, very, extra-very loud, which startles my ears. A lump bumps up in my throat. Then I ask a question that I am almost too afraid to ask.

“What’s over?”

“Everything!”

Twenty-four

Hopper

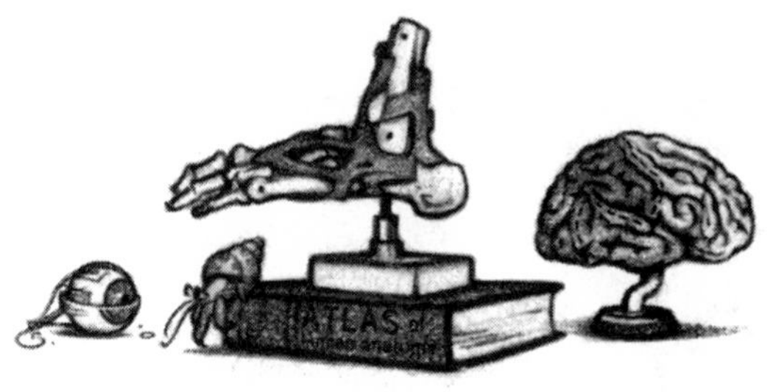

Quinny is no good at taking no for an answer.

She stands on the other side of my door, huffing and puffing, *please*-ing and *why*-ing.

But I don't want to see her right now. I don't want to play, or draw Mr. McSoren on a poster, or hear about her new backpack. I don't even want to *think* about school supplies.

So I use my biggest, most awful voice to make her go away.

From my window, I watch Quinny shuffle home, dragging her new backpack and that poster behind her. I know I hurt her feelings. I should have told her that Trevor and Ty are

coming home from camp today. That's why I can't play. My brothers will be home any minute. But that's not the whole truth of why I can't play. It's just half.

The other half is worse.

I guess she'll find out soon enough. Everything will change in a couple of weeks. And not just because my brothers will be home. When fall starts and school starts and the whole truth starts, Quinny will see the real me. And she won't want to be friends with that person.

Nobody does.

Twenty-five

Quinny

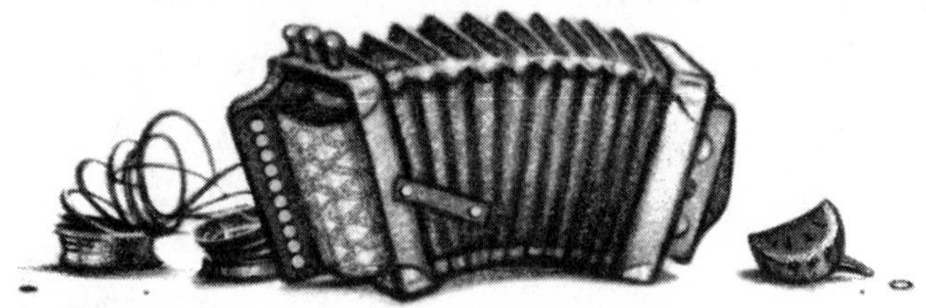

Maybe I *am* stupid. I thought that boy was my friend.

What did I do wrong? And what does he have against my new backpack, anyway? I'm not going to sniffle about it, that's for sure. No matter how leaky my nose feels.

As I walk home, a big, shiny black car whooshes past me on the street. Its windows are so dark that I can't even see who's inside. The car stops in front of Mrs. Porridge's house and out steps a girl wearing the glitteriest pair of sneakers ever, plus sparkly silver tights and a swishy pink and black striped dress. She stands there for a second, like she's posing for a camera.

It's Victoria. And this time I don't accidentally spray her with a freezing water hose. This time I just stare. Did I mention she's carrying a purse made of pink feathers?

I guess Victoria has forgiven me for soaking her with the hose, because she actually walks over to me. "Good morning," she says. "Quinny, right? What are you doing with that poster?"

I glance down at my blank poster and then back at Hopper's house. "Nothing, I guess."

"Could you give it to me, then? I need it for something important."

Before I know it, Victoria swoops the poster right out of my hand.

"Thanks a bunch," she calls out as she walks back toward Mrs. Porridge's house.

That big, shiny black car zooms away now, without even saying good-bye.

I follow Victoria a little. "Hey, wait . . . what are you going to do with my poster?"

She makes a mysterious little half smile. "You'll see."

Then she goes right into Mrs. Porridge's house and shuts the door behind her.

So I guess I won't see.

But a moment later the door opens, and Victoria sticks her head back out. "By the way, I like your backpack."

"You do?" I feel my whole face smiling now.

"It's not pink," she says. "But it's supercute anyway."

"Thanks. Sorry I soaked your dress with the hose."

Walter the cat hisses at me from Mrs. Porridge's front steps.

"You too, Walter. Sorry I soaked your fur."

"I just got that dress," Victoria sighs. "It was a special present from my dad."

It was? I had no idea.

"He bought it in London," she adds. "From a store they don't even have here."

"I'm very, very, extra-very sorry."

"That's okay," says Victoria. "Maybe you

could make it up to me by doing something nice, and then we can be friends."

I nod eagerly.

"That watermelon barrette you're wearing is really cool," she says next. "I've been looking for a barrette just like that for a long time."

I touch the watermelon barrette that's up in my hair. Santa stuffed it into my stocking three years ago. It still smells like watermelon, and it's so comfy that I wear it all the time.

But the way Victoria is looking at it now makes me nervous.

"You're so glamorous," I tell her. "Isn't this fruity barrette kind of babyish for you?"

"Not at all," says Victoria. "It's fun and retro. And it's my favorite shade of pink."

I have no idea what *retro* means, but I do know something about colors.

"Hey, Victoria, you know, this barrette isn't even pink," I point out. "It's red."

"Watermelon insides are reddish-rosy-pink, which is still pink," she insists.

She's wrong about that. But I want Victoria

to know I'm sorry. I want to find out what she's going to do with my poster and where on earth she got a purse made of pink feathers. I want us to be real friends.

So, very sadly, very slowly, I take off the watermelon barrette and hand it to her.

Victoria clicks my barrette into her own hair, then pulls a mirror out of her feathery purse and admires herself. "Thanks! I knew this would look fantastic on me!"

Being generous is supposed to make you feel good. But all I feel right now is confused. Without my favorite barrette, my hair zigzags down in front of my eyes. I try to push it back behind my ears, where it doesn't like to stay for long.

Victoria admires herself for a long time and then snaps her mirror shut, which makes a really loud noise that startles me. "Okay, now we can play," she says.

Fabulous! Except Victoria doesn't want to help me catch Freya. "Who cares about a crazy old chicken?" She doesn't want to play fortune-teller, either. She doesn't even know what a smelling bee is, poor thing, and when I tell her, she says, "Gross!"

Victoria wants to play fashion show.

"We'll start by pulling together some outfits," she says. "Then we'll set up chairs and make a runway. My great-aunt said you're from New York, right? Let's go check out your closet."

"I've got a better idea. Let's dress Walter up for a cat fashion show! I bet that would cheer him up. C'mon, my mom's got some goofy hats we could use. . . ."

I take Victoria's hand and lead her toward my house.

"My great-aunt would never approve of that," she says.

"Or we could have a zombie fashion show! Paint our faces green and walk around moaning and snarling—"

"It's not even Halloween."

"I know—that's the great thing! People will think we're real zombies and be extra scared!"

As we walk up to my front door, Piper pops out from behind a tree, like she always does.

Barefoot, shirtless, dirty, and with a finger up her nose.

"What's that?" Victoria asks.

"That's my little sister Piper."

"What's wrong with her?"

"She's four."

Piper follows us into the house. And up the stairs, toward my room.

Victoria looks back at Piper like she's a walking germ. "On second thought, let's go back to my great-aunt's house," she says. "We'll have more privacy there." Then she calls out, "Mrs. Bumble, Quinny wants to come have lunch with me!"

I do? Victoria sounds so sure, but I don't remember her even asking me.

Mom's busy on the phone, but she waves back a yes. Victoria grabs my hand and pulls me down the stairs. "Come on, I have a surprise for you, too."

"A surprise?" Piper asks, all excited, as she follows us. My little sister loves surprises.

"Sorry, no babies allowed," Victoria says with a sniff.

"Yeah." I smile down at my filthy little twit-ster.

Victoria pulls me along some more. I turn back and see Piper's disappointed face watching us walk away.

I don't know what Victoria's surprise is, but here is another surprise that is truly surprising: seeing Victoria be rude to Piper doesn't feel good.

In fact, it almost makes me want to go back and hug my little sister. Almost.

On our way to Mrs. Porridge's house, Victoria and I pass by Hopper's house. I look up at his window. No one looks back out at me. So I pause for just a second, in case he is about to look out. I think about juggling. And feet. And that beautiful-weird picture book of body parts Hopper likes so much. I think about Freya. Who will help me catch her now?

"Quinny, hurry up," calls Victoria.

One of my feet wants to keep following Victoria toward the exciting surprise, but the other foot wants to go find out why Hopper was being such a crabby-pants before.

"Victoria, wait, I have a better idea. . . ."

But before I can explain, a minivan pulls into Hopper's driveway, and Trevor and Ty burst out of it. Those beastly bully twins are back from summer camp! They run into their yard and pull that soccer goalie net out from behind the garage.

The one that broke, all by itself, when Hopper and I turned it into a hammock.

Uh-oh.

I turn and run to catch up with Victoria. Spending the afternoon safe inside Mrs. Porridge's house suddenly sounds like the best idea after all.

Twenty-six

Hopper

My brothers get home from camp, all rough and loud and covered with mosquito bites. They're furious about their broken soccer net. They're curious about who broke it. Which means they find me (hiding under my bed) and swing me around by my ankles.

But I keep quiet. I'm not tattling on Quinny, no matter what.

Mom finally comes in and makes them stop.

"Boys, that's enough. Sometimes things just break," she says, looking at me like she knows how this particular thing broke. "That's called life. Now stop this nonsense and come downstairs for lunch."

"We know it was you." Trevor pokes me in the chest.

"This isn't over," hisses Ty.

It never is.

"Lunch. Now," Mom reminds us.

"I want pigs in a blanket!" shouts Trevor.

"I want chicken nuggets and fries!" roars Ty.

Mom serves them turkey sandwiches and carrot chips instead. My brothers are so busy whining about the healthy lunch that they forget to keep bothering me. I sit all the way at the other end of the kitchen table. I finish eating my cauliflower sandwich and look out the window.

That's when I notice Quinny walking down the street with Victoria Porridge.

Wait a second.

Victoria only talks to people she can boss. I didn't think anybody could boss Quinny. I watch the two of them walk away. It looks like they're headed toward Mrs. Porridge's house. It looks like they're friends now.

I think I just lost my appetite.

Victoria Porridge never says hi to me, but she's being nice to Quinny. Most people are nice to Quinny, I think. She makes friends wherever she goes. She'll be fine without me when school starts. I'm the one who won't be fine without her.

Because the whole truth is this: I have no friends at school.

None, as in zero.

I used to have a friend, Owen, who I met in kindergarten. Owen built birdhouses out of toothpicks and ate cauliflower sandwiches for lunch and never went anywhere without his pocket dictionary. But he moved away after first grade. And then in second grade, I didn't find anyone else to like who also liked me back.

Of course, there were some friendly grown-ups at school. My second-grade teacher, Mrs. Santos, was kind. The librarian and the lunch lady always said hi. And some of the kids were okay. But there is a big difference between finding an okay kid and finding a true friend. A true friend saves you a seat at lunch, and no one did. A true friend asks, "Where were you?" if you were absent, and no one did. A true friend invites you to his birthday party, and no one did (except for Liam Crewson, who invited the whole class because his parents made him).

I don't know why, but none of the kids at school really noticed me last year. And Victoria Porridge is the one who didn't notice me the most.

Once Quinny finds all this out, she won't be my friend anymore. After all, who wants to be friends with someone who doesn't have any friends?

I finish my sandwich, by hiding most of it under a napkin. Trevor and Ty are wrestling on the floor now. Mom is talking on her phone. I go upstairs without anyone noticing.

I look out my window. From up here I can see Mrs. Porridge's house. I can see Quinny and Victoria standing by the front door, talking.

And talking.

Quinny doesn't look up at me. Not even once.

Finally she and Victoria go inside Mrs. Porridge's house together.

And I pull my window shade down. For good.

Twenty-seven

Quinny

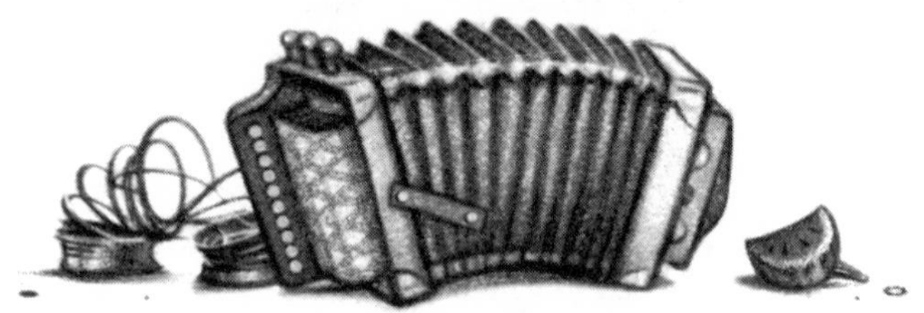

The list of things I learn about Victoria during our walk to Mrs. Porridge's house is very, very, extra-very long.

1) Victoria doesn't have a nickname. (I do. Quinny is short for Quinston, which is actually my middle name.)

2) Victoria is an only child. (Lucky duck.)

3) Victoria owns twenty-seven dresses in her closet, six of which she made herself at a place called fashion camp. (I only have three dresses, and I don't know how to sew my own clothes at all—maybe Victoria can teach me!)

4) Victoria carries a purse everywhere . . . "just in case." (I have just-in-case pockets.)

5) Victoria's purse is not made out of chicken feathers. It is made out of marabou, whatever that is, and she made it herself (also at fashion camp), and everyone loves it so much that she is going to start a business selling marabou purses (plus headbands) and become rich and famous. (I don't know much about purses or headbands, but that last part sounds exciting.)

6) Victoria is going to be in Ms. Yoon's third-grade class at Whisper Valley Elementary School this fall, along with me and Hopper. (Yippee? I hope so.)

7) Victoria is allergic to everything . . . dairy, nuts, and nature. (I'm allergic to nothing, not even dust bunnies—I used to have a bunch of them under my bed back in New York, and we got along great.)

8) Victoria loves to talk about Victoria. (I love to talk about anything.)

The list of things Victoria learns about me on the way to Mrs. Porridge's house is very, very, extra-very short. Because, actually, I don't get a chance to say much. See #8 on the list.

When we get to Mrs. Porridge's front door, Victoria says, "Quinny, close your eyes."

I close them. I hear her opening her purse. I feel her putting something on my wrist.

"Now open your eyes," says Victoria.

I open them. I look down at a bracelet on my wrist. It's itchy-pink, just like the one on Victoria's wrist. "Surprise! It's a friendship bracelet. You're my BFF now."

BFF = best friends forever.

I'm about to say I already have one of those, and he lives right next door to me. But then I remember that maybe I don't anymore.

"BFFs never ever take their friendship bracelets off," says Victoria. "And when school starts, we'll sit together at lunch and play at recess every day. I'll introduce you to everyone and show you the ropes."

"The ropes?"

Before I can ask Victoria what the ropes are, or whether you can have two BFFs at the same time, she pulls me inside Mrs. Porridge's house.

There's no one in the kitchen and no food on

the table. But there's someone out back in the garden.

"Aunt Myrna, we're here!" Victoria calls out. Aunt Myrna is the name Victoria calls Mrs. Porridge, since she is her great-aunt. "What's for lunch?"

"You're looking at it," says Mrs. Porridge, working in her garden between the carrots and the peppers. "Well, don't just stand there, help yourselves."

I've heard of a salad bar, but Mrs. Porridge's garden bar is different. We pick our lunch from the ground. We pick peppers. We pick zucchini. We pick carrots and eggplant and heart-shaped tomatoes. I do most of the picking because Victoria doesn't want to get her hands dirty since she is allergic to dirt.

"That's ridiculous, Victoria," says Mrs. Porridge. "You are not allergic to topsoil."

Then we go back inside and wash up, and Mrs. Porridge cooks all the veggies in a big, sizzly pan. And then she stuffs them into chewy-crispy-warm tortillas, which are green—my favorite color! For dessert, Mrs. Porridge slices strawberries on top of peach ice cream. It's soy ice cream, since Victoria is allergic to dairy, and it actually tastes pretty good.

After lunch, Victoria opens this giant box of stuff she keeps at her great-aunt's house. It's full of jewelry and hair accessories and flavored lip glosses and nail polish. Wow. Everything in here is so neat and shiny and perfect. Nothing looks chewed or broken, or sticky with little-sister spit and boogers. Victoria is so lucky.

"I love painting nails," I tell Victoria. "Do you have any green?"

"Why in the world would I have green nail polish?"

"It's my favorite color."

"Quinny, nobody paints their nails green. Here, you're going to paint mine POPSICLE PINK, and then I'll paint yours FUSCHIA FOREVER."

I try. But Victoria's fingernails are so small and dainty, I keep painting outside the nails.

"Quinny, be careful!"

Victoria stops me and paints the rest of her own nails, all neat and perfect.

Then she starts painting mine. “Don’t move,” she orders me. “Sit perfectly still!”

But when my body has to sit still, my brain moves around a whole lot extra to make up for it. I wonder again what “the ropes” are. I wonder again if a person can have two “best friends forever” at the same time.

Out loud I wonder, "I wonder what Hopper is doing right now."

"Who?"

"The boy next door. I mean, he lives next door to me . . . in that gingerbread house."

I don't mention that he is the same boy who helped me soak Victoria's dry-clean-only dress with the freezing water hose. And I don't mention how rude Hopper was to me earlier today. For some reason, I feel like giving that boy a second chance.

Victoria shrugs and keeps polishing my nails all neat and careful until they are FUSCHIA FOREVER.

"Maybe we should invite him over," I say.

"Who?"

"Hopper. The boy I was just talking about."

Victoria stops painting my nails and looks up at me. "Quinny, grow up."

"I'm working on it."

"Hopper is a boy."

"So?"

"So boys are messy and annoying."

"Not Hopper. And you should see him juggle!"

"Well, I'm sorry. You can't just go around playing with boys in third grade. It's not normal."

"But I played with lots of boys last year."

"That was last year. Second grade is just for practice. Third grade is when real life begins."

"It is?"

"In third grade, you get your own real locker and nobody sits on the carpet anymore for stories, and nobody's allowed to cry anymore, and the girls eat lunch with the girls and the boys eat lunch with the boys, and there's no more just playing tag with everybody in a big group, and if you play with a boy at recess, it means you want to kiss him on the lips."

"What?!"

"If you don't believe me, go ask my cousin Janie."

I feel wobbly inside my chest. I feel woozy inside my nose. It might be from the stink of all that nail polish. I scratch at my wrist and wonder if I am allergic to itchy-pink.

"Quinny, are you okay?" says Mrs. Porridge

from across the room. "You look a little green."

I wish.

Then the big, shiny black car comes back for Victoria and honks its horn. Whoever is driving that thing doesn't even come inside the house—Victoria just goes outside all by herself.

"Be careful with your nails," she says as she leaves. "And don't take that bracelet off or get it dirty. I'll be at fashion camp all next week, but I'll come back to play again before school starts, I promise."

Then Mrs. Porridge walks me home. On the way, she looks at me all suspicious.

"Quinny, are you sure you're all right?"

I'm fine. Except I didn't know that my real life hasn't started yet. I didn't know you aren't allowed to cry in third grade and you can't play with boys unless you want to kiss them on the lips. I don't even know what "the ropes" are, and it's too late to ask Victoria.

I wonder if Hopper knows.

Then I realize, of course he does. He has older bully twin brothers, so he must know all about these third-grade rules. (Having older kids in your family is like being able to see into the future.) I think about how Trevor and Ty made those teasing kissy-poo noises when they first saw me and Hopper playing together, and how Hopper suddenly stopped being friendly when the back-to-school letter arrived, and how he yelled at me that everything's over. It all makes sense now. My heart does a forward roll down into my stomach. I don't want everything to be over. But now, thanks to Victoria, I know for sure that it is.

Twenty-eight

Hopper

I decide to go back to my regular life from before I ever met Quinny. I've got plenty of things to keep me busy. For example:

I juggle my knives—special juggling knives with dull blades that can't cut.

I put together a second foot-skeleton model, so now I have a pair of feet on my shelf.

I sharpen my set of charcoal pencils to their sharpest points ever and draw a sketch of Freya the chicken. I haven't heard her clucking by Quinny's house lately. I wonder why not.

I ride my bike to the town pool with Grandpa Gooley and swim dozens of laps.

Hundreds, probably.

Two days go by like this.

On the third day of not talking to Quinny, I peek out my window and see her playing Chutes and Ladders on her bed with her little sister Piper. Then I stop peeking in case she notices.

On the fourth day of not talking to Quinny, I watch Quinny get into her car with her whole family. They're all wearing swimsuits. I know this is the last week that the town pool is open. The last real week of summer. But I'm not going swimming if she'll be there. Instead I spend the day in my room, playing chess against myself. And putting together a four-hundred-piece puzzle of the human heart. And juggling. I wonder, were Quinny and I ever friends in the first place? Maybe she's just nice to everyone and I misunderstood. Maybe this summer felt too good to be true because it wasn't true.

On the fifth day of not talking to Quinny, Mom comes into my room and dumps a big pile of clothes on my dresser. It's that time again. Every year, before school starts, I try on Trevor's and Ty's old clothes to see what finally fits me.

I don't mind wearing my brothers' hand-me-downs. In fact I kind of like it. When I try on Trevor's and Ty's old clothes, it feels like something new might happen to me, like maybe I'll turn big and loud and strong and not afraid of anything, just like my brothers.

I pull on one of Trevor's old shirts. I zip up a pair of Ty's old shorts.

I look in the mirror. I look the same. My personality feels the same.

I guess they're just clothes, not magic clothes.

"Hopper, we're leaving for the mall in fifteen minutes!" calls Mom.

I knew this was coming. Back-to-school shopping. Since I don't need new stuff, I don't see why I have to get dragged to the mall just because Trevor and Ty do.

"Can't I stay home this time?"

"Hopper, you're not old enough to stay home by yourself. Plus, you need a haircut."

We drive to the mall. The problem is, Trevor and Ty get as bored shopping for clothes as I do. And when my brothers get bored, they get mean.

In the mall's parking lot, Trevor walks behind me a little and keeps stepping on my heel. On purpose. But every time I turn around, he makes an innocent smile.

"Stop it," I tell him.

"Stop what?"

Later we sit at the food court with pizza, and when mom isn't looking, Ty flicks my ear.

"Stop it," I tell him.

"Stop what?"

He does it again. And again. Finally I turn around and punch him in the stomach.

Hard.

Mom is shocked. "Hopper, what's gotten into you?"

I don't know. I've never punched anyone in my life. I didn't even know that I knew how to punch—it just happened. And it felt good.

I expect Ty to hit me back, but he laughs instead. Trevor looks impressed.

But mom is not impressed.

"Hopper, that is unacceptable behavior. Please apologize to your brother."

"What for? He never apologizes to me."

"Hopper, we don't punch people in this family!"

"Sure we do. Where have you been?"

"Apologize to your brother—"

"He's not even hurt."

"—or you're not getting ice cream!"

"I don't care!"

"Hopper!"

"Leave me alone!"

I run away from Mom. From everything.

I run and run. I feel angry and angrier and angriest. I hide behind a big display of suitcases. Maybe if I squeeze myself into one of these suitcases someone will buy it and take me home to a different family without Trevor and Ty and without a mother who treats them better than she treats me.

Mom finds me before that can happen. She marches me back to the car. But we don't go

LIMITED TIME
CLEARANCE!
for savings up to 75%
end of summer
SALE
65%
GET AWAY

home yet. "You can't go back to school without a haircut," she reminds me.

Great.

She takes us all to Kidz Cutz, where I have to sit in a tall chair with a scratchy black cape strangling my neck. I like my head just the way it is, but a happy haircutter-lady picks up a loud electric razor and starts buzzing my hair off.

All of it.

That buzzy razor scares my skin. It makes the back of my neck itchy.

"So, Hopper, how do you like your new haircut?" the happy haircutter-lady asks.

My ears feel windy now and my forehead feels too bare. I look at myself in the mirror. It's like a whole layer of me is gone.

"I hate it," I tell her.

At home, I'm still not sorry for punching my brother and running off and being rude to the happy haircutter-lady at Kidz Cutz, so Mom grounds me to my room.

"Fine with me!" I run upstairs and slam the door behind me.

"Hopper, is this really how you want to end the summer?" Mom calls out.

Actually, yes, it is. I'd rather be up in my room by myself than anywhere else. I wish everyone would just leave me alone forever. Mom and Dad have each other to bug. Trevor and Ty have each other to pound on. And Quinny has Victoria.

Just in case Mom tries to come in and talk to me, I hide under my bed. But then I notice that sketch of Quinny is still under here, the one I drew of her in the middle of the night right after we met. I barely remember drawing it. It was a stupid thing to do.

I reach out and rip that sketch of Quinny.

I rip it right down the middle of her smile.

Twenty-nine

Quinny

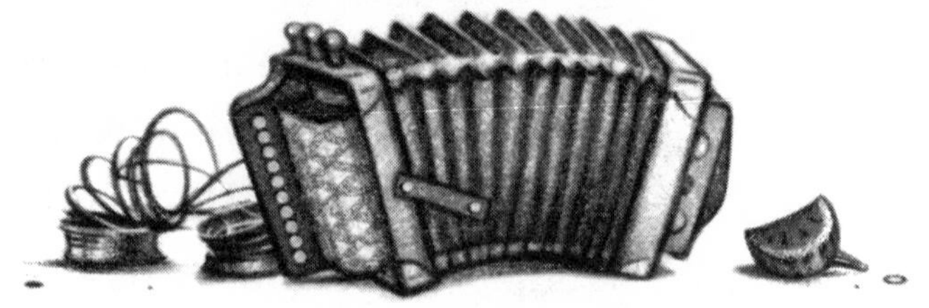

Hopper's window shade has been closed tight all week, and it's hard for me to pretend I don't care. But the more you practice something, the better you get at it, so after a few days I become very, very, extra-very talented at ignoring that boy who is ignoring me. I don't even bother peeking out at his house anymore. I pretend that window is a wall.

Victoria is busy with her last week of fashion camp before school starts, so I spend my time playing with Piper. On Wednesday we play Candy Land until Piper cheats, on Thursday we play Chutes and Ladders until Piper cheats, and on Friday we play Crazy Eights until Piper cheats.

On Saturday, because I'm totally bored of Piper cheating, I offer to babysit Cleo, even while she isn't napping. That baby drools and bites and pulls my hair. But then I make her do this fun trick where she burps and farts at the same time. All you have to do is feed her a broccoli smoothie, wait five minutes, then squeeze her right below her belly button. Not every baby can do it, but Cleo's special.

Mom sees me playing with Cleo and looks at me all funny. "Quinny, what's going on?"

"Nothing."

"Why are you suddenly being so nice to your sisters?"

"I thought you wanted me to be nice to them."

"What I mean is, why aren't you playing with Hopper these days?"

"He's got other plans." It must be true, since he and I don't have any plans together.

I hear a noise coming from Hopper's driveway

and glance outside. There he is, getting out of his car with his mom. I haven't seen Hopper all week. His hair is much shorter now and his head looks so different—like it shrank in the dryer or something. He doesn't even look like Hopper anymore. He looks like a stranger. A very scowly stranger.

"Did you guys have a fight or something?" Mom asks.

Or something.

"Well, things have certainly been a lot calmer without the two of you running around trying to catch that chicken. Freya's been pretty quiet lately, hasn't she?"

Freya has been quiet. Too quiet. My heart hurts when I think about her. So I try not to.

The day before school starts, Victoria comes back to visit me, just like she threatened—I mean, promised. From upstairs I see her knock on my front door. Then I look down at my hands. My FUSCHIA FOREVER nails are chipped and my

BFF bracelet is dirty. I run into my room and shut my door tight.

"I think I have a cold," I tell Mom when she comes upstairs to say I have a guest.

"You don't sound sick," she says.

"Well, I should get ready for school. Piper and I need to take a bath."

"A bath?" says Victoria, who comes upstairs right behind Mom. "With your little sister, the dirty one who pees outside? Gross. Baths are for babies, anyway. I take showers all by myself, like a normal third grader."

Another crummy third-grade rule.

Victoria walks into my room and sits down on my bed. "Well, I finally finished it," she says, holding up my poster board, which isn't blank anymore. Now it's all swirly and bright and it says, "Magnificent Marabou Creations from ViP Fashions. Victoria Porridge, President and Designer in Chief." And it has pictures of the fluffiest, sneeziest, most itchy-pink purses and headbands I've ever seen.

"Alice at the dry cleaners said I could put this up in her window, to advertise my new business," says Victoria. "You can be my first customer! Do you prefer hot pink or dusty rose? I custom-dye all the marabou feathers myself. Quinny, wake up. Are you listening to me?"

I'm trying to.

"Accessories are just the beginning," she says. "Soon I'll branch out into dresses. My counselor at fashion camp helped me put together a business plan. I'm going to build a whole fashion empire and make millions!"

Wow. Victoria knows how to think big. She looks so proud of herself, for something that hasn't even happened yet.

I show her my tap-dance shoes, because they are the most stylish things I own and Victoria is very stylish. "Those make too much noise," she says. "I take ballet."

Next I show her my accordion. Maybe she likes music, too. "That thing looks so heavy," she says. "I play the flute."

Then Victoria spots some of Piper's books on

my floor. "I can't believe you still read picture books," she says.

"Only to my little sisters." I push those babyish books beneath my bed. "They're not even mine." (Except for sometimes, when I still look at them a little bit.)

"Well, I read *real* books," Victoria says. "Chapter books and novels. My favorite one is called *Ballet Shoes* and I've read it, like, a million times."

Before I get a chance to tell Victoria what my favorite book is, she opens my closet and pokes around in there. She turns back to me, looking confused.

"Is your mother doing laundry today?"

"I doubt it." Daddy does the laundry in our family.

"So where's all your new stuff?" she asks. "Didn't you go shopping for school?"

"I did. I got a notebook and pencils and—"

"No silly, I meant clothes shopping."

"I already have clothes. I'm going to wear my favorite green skirt tomorrow and my favorite

T-shirt, which actually used to be my mom's. She wore it the night she met my daddy at this Paul McCartney concert a long time ago, plus I'm wearing my favorite fruity kneesocks—"

"Quinny," Victoria sighs, "I don't mean grubby old play clothes. I mean real clothes. Brand-new back-to-school outfits."

"You mean like school uniforms?" We had those at my old school. I hated them.

Victoria sighs again. She looks at me like maybe I'm not as smart as she is.

"You'll see when you get there," she says. "Your parents are driving you, right? You're not riding that awful school bus, I hope."

Actually, I am riding that awful school bus. "Why is the school bus awful?" I ask.

"You'll see."

I'll see what? I'm so confused. We're supposed to be playing, but this is no fun at all.

I don't know what to say next, which almost never happens. But then I think of something. "Did you know that Hopper's going to be in the same class as us?"

Victoria sighs again. She must have a lot of air in her head. "Didn't know and don't care."

"Me neither. I haven't talked to that boy all week."

"Good. You know, you only played with him because there was no one else around."

That's one reason I played with Hopper. But it's not the only reason.

"Now you have me," Victoria says. "We're going to have a great year together."

I hope so. But it kind of almost feels like Victoria is trying to put me on a leash, and I kind of almost want to run away. Except, where would I go? Hopper isn't my friend anymore. And I don't know any other kids in this too-small town.

So I try to keep playing with Victoria. And I try very, very, extra-very hard to keep forgetting about Hopper, just like he's forgotten about me.

By the time Victoria leaves, I am exhausted from all that trying. And from all her rules.

Baths < showers.

Tap dance < ballet.

Accordion < flute.

Picture books < chapter books.

Play clothes < brand-new back-to-school outfits.

Riding the bus < getting driven to school in a shiny black car.

It's starting to feel like: Quinny <<< Victoria.

"Cheer up, honey," says Mom. "You'll see Victoria in school tomorrow."

Fabulous.

And then my life gets even worse. Because I notice icky-sticky-screamy Cleo sitting on my brand-new green polka-dot backpack. And she's holding a purple marker. And she's trying to connect the dots!

"Cleo, stop!"

Instead of stopping, that baby hurries to scribble some more.

"Mom, make her stop!"

Mom grabs Cleo and plops her in the Pack 'n Play. "Cleo, that was inappropriate," she says in a way-too-calm voice.

We scrub my backpack. Some of the marker comes out, but most of it doesn't.

"Honey, I'm sorry," Mom says. "But Cleo's just a baby."

I know that. I try very, very, extra-very hard to not blame Cleo for being just a baby.

At bedtime, I'm still trying. Mom helps me set out my grubby, not-new play clothes for school tomorrow morning. She helps me fill my stained backpack with pencils and a plain notebook.

When germy, babyish Piper comes by to get me for our bath, I slam my door in her face.

Then I peek out my window. Hopper's window shade is still closed. I close mine, too.

This was supposed to be my luckiest summer ever.

But it's the night before school starts, and I'm all out of good luck.

Thirty

Hopper

Trevor and Ty are carpooling to middle school with their soccer friends this morning. But I'll be taking the bus to third grade, just like I did to second grade.

I like riding the school bus. It's higher up than our minivan, so you can see more. And Ms. Kray, the bus aide, always assigns me a seat near the middle, where nothing too loud or terrible goes on. But this year I'm nervous because Quinny is going to be on my bus, and she is not talking to me anymore and I am not talking to her. Everything has changed. Everything.

After breakfast, Mom walks me to the corner.

We stand there and wait for the bus. And for Quinny.

Here she comes.

Her hair's gotten bigger, like Aunt LuAnne's Chia Pet, and she's not wearing her watermelon barrette for some reason. Behind all that hair, her eyes don't even peek at mine. Neither do her teeth, because her mouth is closed. She's got her hands shoved in her pockets, but she keeps taking them out to scratch at a bracelet on her wrist.

Now she's right in front of me. Close enough to touch.

Does she think my new haircut looks awful?

Does she miss me even a tiny bit?

I am not brave enough to look Quinny in the face, so I look her in the socks. Her socks are so long that they come all the way up to her knees. Her right sock is green with big orange dots, which I think are supposed to be orange slices. Her left sock is orange with green dots, which are apples. One of the apples has a worm coming out of it. The worm is smiling.

I'm not sure how long a person can stare at girls' socks, but I think I might have broken the world record for it. The problem is, I don't know what else to do. We are the only kids at this bus stop. Mom and Quinny's mom are busy yakking on about *contractors* and *property taxes* and *class size*. Nobody seems to care that Quinny and I are not saying a word to each other.

Nobody except me.

The school bus finally pulls up to our corner. I hug Mom good-bye and follow Quinny's socks up the steps.

Then there is another problem. Ms. Kray on the bus always gives us assigned seats, and this year she puts me and Quinny together in a two-seater near the back. I don't want to sit near the back of the bus. I don't want to sit next to Quinny, either. But she scoots right into the seat, without complaining. I look up at Ms. Kray for help, but I guess she doesn't know what my face means, because she goes back to her own seat. I hear the bus engine rumble. I have no choice but to sit next to Quinny.

Quinny buckles her seat belt. I buckle mine. She pulls her backpack away and hides it behind her feet, like she doesn't want me anywhere near it. Then she turns her head all the way toward the window and keeps it there. I can't even see her cheeks.

It feels like the longest bus ride ever. I've never been so happy to get to school in my life.

I follow the crowd of kids into the building and find my new third-grade classroom. I meet my teacher, Ms. Yoon. She smiles hello at me, but I hardly notice her face, because her belly is enormous. It's so huge that Ms. Yoon walks like an Oompa-Loompa from *Charlie and the Chocolate Factory*. A tall, friendly, tired-looking Oompa-Loompa. Either Ms. Yoon had a really big breakfast or there's a baby inside her belly.

I find my cubby, which has a door this year, so it's called a locker. Quinny's locker is all the way down the hall. Fine with me.

I find my desk. Quinny's desk is all the way across the classroom. Good.

We all sit down, and Ms. Yoon tells us who

she is again. Then she makes us go around and introduce our names, so the whole class can hear. A few kids are brand-new this year, like Quinny. Most kids are old news, like me. I know almost everybody here and they know me, and we all know that I don't play with anyone except Owen and that since he moved away, I just sit and read during recess. Pretty soon Quinny will find out, too. But I don't care, since we're not friends anymore.

Then Ms. Yoon starts talking about school stuff. But before she can get very far, Quinny raises her hand. "Ms. Yoon, there's a baby in your tummy, isn't there?" she asks.

"Why, yes, Eleanor, I was just about to get to that," says Ms. Yoon.

"Actually, everyone calls me Quinny, remember? Hey, can you still tie your shoes?"

Some kids in the class laugh at this. I'm not one of them.

"Pardon?" says Ms. Yoon.

"It must be hard for you to bend down," Quinny says. "Can you even *see* your shoes?"

"Does it hurt?" blurts out a boy.

"When will the baby be born?" asks another girl.

I have a question of my own—*Can you feel the baby's heart beating in your belly the way you feel your own heart beat in your chest?*—but I don't feel comfortable asking it out loud.

"Are you going to bring the baby to school?" asks Quinny.

"I already do—every day," Ms. Yoon says, with a tired smile now.

"What are you going to name it?" asks another girl.

"You should name it Victoria if it's a girl," says Victoria.

"My dog's name is Brutus," says a boy.

"My gerbil's name is Sweet Potato," says a girl.

"My chicken's name was Freya," sighs Quinny.

I hear the sadness in her voice. *Freya.* For a second I feel it, too. We worked so hard to catch that chicken. We came so close.

"All right, class, that's enough." Ms. Yoon chuckles. "The baby will be born later this year, and we haven't picked out a name yet. Let's move on. . . ."

Ms. Yoon starts talking about schedules and textbooks, and everybody settles down and the day goes on. We get new writing journals. We play basketball addition in math, which we did last year, too, so I already know how. We get in line to go to library.

"Hopper, look how you've grown!" says Mr. Brolin, the school librarian.

It's true. Now I can reach up to the top shelf, where all the fifth-grade books are.

After library, we get in line and go to gym.

"Hopper! Wow, I almost didn't recognize you!" says Ms. Demming, the gym teacher.

Now I can climb the rock wall without a boost. I start climbing and keep climbing. I reach the top and look out over the whole gym. Everyone looks so small from up here. So quiet. So harmless. Even Quinny.

I wish I could stay up here forever. But I can't, because after gym we have music.

And after music Ms. Yoon takes us outside for the worst part of the day. Recess.

Thirty-one

Quinny

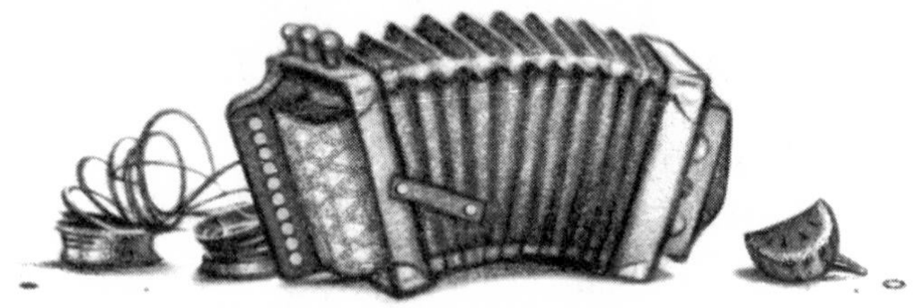

Except for Ms. Yoon's fabulous gigantic baby belly, I don't love third grade at Whisper Valley Elementary School so far. Here's why:

Riding the bus this morning with a rude boy who ignored me was a frowny way to start the day. (I'm not going to waste my breath talking about him, but his name starts with an *H*.)

And then we got off the bus, and the school was so big and I wasn't sure where to go, and I wished someone would help me (the boy whose name starts with an *H*, for example), but no one did. All the grown-ups were busy helping the smaller kids, I noticed. The bigger you are, the more people think you know where you're going, but that's not always true. Finally a teacher pointed the way, and I found my classroom and it wasn't that hard, but I didn't know that ahead of time, so I was just a little bit scared.

And then my locker wouldn't open right, or close right. Cubbies were much easier!

And then Victoria showed up, wearing a glittery itchy-pink top and a puffy itchy-pink skirt and my favorite watermelon barrette that I gave her by mistake. She saw my backpack and made a crinkly face.

"You can't bring a dirty, ruined backpack to third grade," she said. "Get rid of that thing."

I looked down at Cleo's marker scribbles on my backpack. I thought: *ruined* is kind of a mean word. Especially the way Victoria said it. Cleo was probably just trying to draw a tree.

"I can't get rid of it," I told Victoria. "Mom and Dad just got it for me."

"Tell them you want a new one. Duh!"

And then Victoria introduced me to all the pretty friends, who belong to her very much, and their names were Kaitlin, Kaylee, and McKayla.

Their backpacks were clean, and their clothes were mostly itchy-pink birthday-party clothes, and their hair was mostly skinny, and their mouths mostly whispered. I noticed they were all wearing BFF bracelets, too.

"I thought you were from New York City," said one of those pretty friends. She looked at me from head to toe, like she was searching for something she couldn't find.

"I am. I mean, I was." I felt a tiny droop of sadness make me shorter.

Those girls all looked at me like they didn't quite believe me.

"That T-shirt's really old," said another pretty friend.

It used to be Mom's from the night she met Daddy. That's why it's special.

"Your socks don't match," said the third pretty friend. "It looks like you got dressed in the dark." And everyone giggled. Except me, because I was the one they were giggling at.

"Well, it looks like you guys got dressed in a bubble-gum factory," I said, not because I was making fun, but because it was plain old true. I'd never seen so much itchy-pink in my life.

Then all those pretty girls looked at me a certain way, and I have never seen girls look at me like that before. It was not pretty. And Victoria smiled, but not in a nice way, either.

Then the bell rang and the classroom part of school started, and I finally got to meet Ms. Yoon and her fabulous gigantic baby belly. I had tons of curious questions about that belly, but I only got to ask a few since we had to rush on to regular-typical stuff like writing and math.

And now writing and math are over, so we're lining up to go to library.

And that's my first day of school so far.

So far, so bad—except for Ms. Yoon's fabulous gigantic baby belly.

Library is when you have to be all quiet, which is not one of my strengths. It is one of Victoria's strengths, I notice. She knows how to be quiet, even when she is talking. Everywhere we go, from library to gym to music, she and those pretty girls whisper into one another's ears. I don't know how to whisper very well. My talking always comes out too big. Whispering is for secrets, and I'm not good at keeping those, either.

Everywhere we go, Victoria also keeps an eye on me. From library to gym to music, she tells me where to sit and what to do and who's who and what's what. All I have to do is obey her and my life will turn out fine. But my body is full of this strange, shaky feeling. Like I'm wearing my sneakers on the wrong feet and my right earlobe is heavier than my left. I rub the skin on the side of my head, right where my watermelon barrette used to be. I think maybe I am having a sad hair day.

In the hallway after music, Victoria hooks her arm through mine and pulls me along. "Come on, we always start by meeting at the sycamore tree," she says. "Then we'll work our way over to the blacktop for jump rope and hula hoops."

It takes me a second to figure out what that girl is talking about.

Recess is next.

Thirty-two

Hopper

I've been going to school since kindergarten and I still don't understand recess. It's too loud and too fast. It's too crowded and too rough. And there's never enough shade.

My friend Owen didn't like recess, either, so we would always play together, away from all the trouble. But then Owen moved away in second grade, so from then on I just sat on the steps at recess and read a book. Some of the playground grown-ups tried to stop me at first. They tried to get me to play tag with the other kids, but I didn't want to. Trevor and Ty chase me around at home all the time. Who needs more of that at school?

Reading on the steps was my kind of fun. So I sat there for second-grade recess and I read *The Great Brain Book* and *Why Don't Your Eyelashes Grow?* and all the Harry Potter books and *The Art of Juggling* and *Dr. Frankenstein's Human Body Book* and *Have a Nice DNA* and *Blood and Guts: A Working Guide to Your Own Insides.* (Grandpa Gooley was amazed by all my reading. "Hopper, you'll make an outstanding doctor one day," he told me. "Or possibly an Olympic swimmer." The reason he said that last part is because we were at the pool during this conversation, and I'd just beaten him in the fifty-meter freestyle.)

This year, in third grade, I don't know what's going to happen at recess.

Hopefully nothing new.

When I get outside, I see that recess is still loud, fast, crowded, and rough. I sit on the steps. I pull out my book. (I'm starting off the school year with *101 Things You Didn't Know about the Human Heart.*) Without moving my head too much, I look around for Quinny. Not because she is my friend, but just to see where she is, so I know where not to look. I see her standing with Victoria and a bunch of Victoria-type girls by the sycamore tree. They're talking in one another's ears and covering their mouths with their hands. But Quinny isn't talking. She doesn't look happy. Which is not my problem, since we're not friends anymore.

Then a strange thing happens.

One of the new kids, a boy named Caleb who moved here from California and who doesn't know yet that I'm not too friendly, runs past and tags me.

"You're it!" Caleb cries as he runs away.

I stand up. "Wait. . . ."

I'm never it. I'm not even in the game. If this new kid knew me, he'd know that.

But Caleb keeps running away.

And then I realize everyone's looking at me. Everyone's waiting.

Suddenly I *am* in the game, even though I don't want to be. I'm it.

I put down my book and walk down the steps.

Everyone runs out of my way because I'm it. But I don't chase anybody.

I walk all the way over to the other side of the playground, to the sycamore tree.

I walk right up to Quinny and I tag her arm.

"You're it."

Thirty-three

Quinny

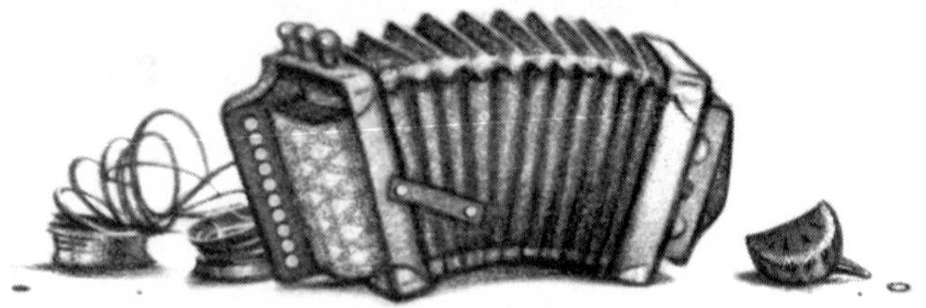

I'm *what*?

I stare at Hopper, very, very, extra-very shocked.

First of all, he isn't even my friend anymore, and second of all, we're not supposed to be playing tag in third grade (although a ton of kids didn't hear about that rule, I guess, and are still playing tag). And third of all, Victoria is watching me, and I don't want to make her mad by playing tag with a boy who is not even my friend anymore.

But here he is, standing right in front of me.

So I tag Hopper back. Hard.

He stands there for a second, like he's surprised, and then he tags me AGAIN.

So I tag him again. And he tags me again.

This keeps happening until Victoria steps between us.

"Leave her alone!" Victoria booms at Hopper, right up his nose, which is the place he is most sensitive about words getting boomed.

Hopper's startled nose backs away from Victoria. He looks at me. It is not a making-fun kind of look.

I don't know what to do now. I'm still mad at him and I'm still sad at him, but I'm also still curious about him.

"Quinny, why are you playing with a boy?" Victoria huffs at me.

"I . . . I . . ."

"Remember the rules."

And then Victoria's mouth makes a terrible kissy shape. The other girls giggle.

"Get him!" Victoria cries.

Two pretty friends grab Hopper's arms and

back him up against the sycamore tree.

Victoria and another pretty friend push me toward Hopper.

"Pucker up, city girl," sneers Victoria.

"No!"

"Kiss him!"

"Do it!"

"On the lips!"

"You love him!"

The pretty friends giggle as they push me toward Hopper now. His face is white. His looking-looking eyes are bulging. Our lips are getting closer.

Hopper's lips + my lips = the biggest vomit volcano in the history of vomit volcanoes.

I shake my head, I close my eyes, I try to swallow my own mouth. This can't be happening. It's just a bad dream.

And then somebody screams.

"KEEE-YAAAAP!"

It's me. And it's called self-defense. A strong, fast side kick to the left. My leg does it without me even realizing.

"Owwww!" screeches Victoria, whose knee gets in the way of my kick.

The other girls move away from me. No one's giggling anymore. They all look afraid. That's right. You mess with a tae kwon do green belt, you should be scared. Very, very, extra-very scared.

"I think you broke my kneecap," Victoria whimpers, limping a little before falling elegantly to the ground. "Call nine-one-one. I need an ambulance—"

"Victoria, I'm so sorry. I didn't mean to—"

"Don't touch me. Shame on you for attacking your best . . ."

But then Victoria stops in the middle of her sentence. Her face gets all stiff.

"Quinny?" she says in a creepy, calm voice.

"What?"

She points up at my bare wrist. "Where's the friendship bracelet I gave you?"

I look at my wrist. I realize that itchy-pink thing must have fallen off.

"What did you do with it?" Victoria snaps.

"You weren't supposed to take it off, ever."

"I didn't."

"Put it back on right now."

I look at the ground all around me, but it's no use. That friendship bracelet is gone. I look around the playground. Hopper's gone, too.

"Quinny, we're waiting!"

Victoria stands up, glaring at me. The good news is, I guess she doesn't need an ambulance after all. The grumpy news is, she's waiting for me to put on something that I don't even have.

The other girls wait for Victoria to finish waiting. Kaylee whispers into Kaitlin's ear. Then Kaitlin whispers into McKayla's ear. All their eyes stare at me in a sunburny way.

I close my eyes and try very, very, extra-very hard to remember the rules again. Especially this one: there's no crying in third grade.

"I'm sorry," I mumble. "I don't know where it is."

"Fine," Victoria huffs.

Then, with a mean little smile, she reaches up to her own head and unsnaps my precious watermelon barrette and throws it over the playground fence.

Thirty-four

Hopper

I'll have to move now. Switch schools. Switch towns. Switch planets. Almost getting kissed on the playground isn't the kind of thing a person can survive.

"Hey, moron, you're still it!"

That's what Alex Delgado shouts at me as I walk back to the steps, where I left my book. I turn to look at him. And I realize he doesn't know. Alex didn't see me getting attacked by that pack of wild girls. No one did. It all happened behind the sycamore tree.

"Hey, moron!" Alex hollers again. "Any day now!"

Alex is the biggest, fastest, toughest boy in my grade. I'm not weird enough for him to tease or sporty enough for him to play sports with, so he usually doesn't pay me any attention. And I'd like to keep it that way. But I guess Alex doesn't know that I'm a pretty fast runner, too, when I bother trying. (The reason: years of practice running away from Trevor and Ty.)

I start running toward Alex Delgado.

He laughs at first. Then he finally starts running away from me. I'm still IT, after all.

Alex runs fast. But I run faster.

It only takes me about five seconds to tag Alex Delgado on the back.

"You're it!"

Alex turns around. He's all mad and sputtering and breathing hard. But it was a fair-and-square tag. Everybody saw it.

He reaches out his hand, but before he can tag me back, I run. I hear Alex's feet pounding the ground behind me. I hear the kids around us yelling and cheering. My legs are burning and my lungs are burning, but I feel good everywhere else and I keep on running.

Alex can't get close enough to tag me.

The recess bell rings, and I run right into the line for my class.

"Till next time," Alex says, trying to catch his breath. "Moron."

But this time he says it with a chuckle. He shoves me in a way that is almost friendly. Then he lines up with his own class and goes back into the building.

And I am kind of amazed that I am still alive.

After all that running, I'm hungry. Which brings me to the second-worst thing about school. Lunch.

In the cafeteria, each classroom has to sit together, and you only get three tables per class. The first table is always full of girls. The second table is full of boys. The third table gets the leftovers—some boys, some girls—and this was where Owen and I would always sit before he moved away. Even though he is gone now, I still sit at the third table. But there is nobody there for me to be quiet with, so I just try my best to eat through all the talking.

And that's the main problem with lunch.

Talking. It would be a lot better if you could just sit there and chew your sandwich in peace. All that conversation is pointless, if you ask me. People say the same stuff over and over again, day after day.

But today, they say something different. And they say it to me.

"I can't believe you tagged Alex."

"That was awesome."

"No one's tagged Alex since first grade."

"Did you see the look on his face?"

"No," I say. "Because he was running away from me."

The kids laugh.

I don't know what all the fuss is about. Playing tag is not as much fun as swimming laps or reading *Blood and Guts* or making body-part models or juggling or correcting the pH level in my fish tank or sketching with charcoal pencils in my own quiet room.

But it might be an okay way to spend recess sometimes. Since I have to be out on the playground anyway.

The other kids keep talking as they clear their lunch trays. So do I.

I can't believe I'm talking at lunch. I can't believe I played with other kids at recess. Maybe I've been taken over by aliens. Or maybe third grade isn't the end of everything. Maybe it's the beginning of something new.

After lunch we go to science. This year we get to do science in a room down in the basement called a laboratory that's all set up with

microscopes and test tubes and goggles and stuff. There's no life-size skeleton in here, but there's a giant poster of one. I think this might be the most interesting place in the whole school.

After science we go to art, where I draw the fastest animal on the planet. Most people think that's a cheetah, but it's not. The fastest animal in the whole world—land, water, and air included—is actually the peregrine falcon, a bird that dives through the sky at more than two hundred miles an hour.

"Holy smoke," says Mr. Duvall, the new art teacher, smiling down at my sketch. "Hopper, I didn't know that. What an amazing creature."

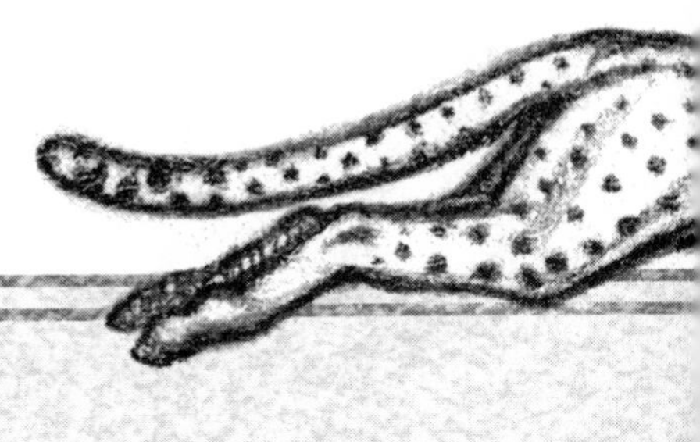

He wants to hang my work on the wall, and I let him.

After art, it's time to go home.

I can't believe the day is over. It feels like I just got here.

We get our backpacks and line up to go outside. Everyone walks out, but I notice something that makes me stop—a pair of big feet sticking out of the very last locker. The person they're attached to looks like she is trying to hide.

I know what trying to hide feels like.

I walk back to the feet. I open the locker door all the way.

Quinny's eyes look up at me. A tear rolls down her cheek and falls into that little hole called a dimple.

PEREGRINE FALCON
200

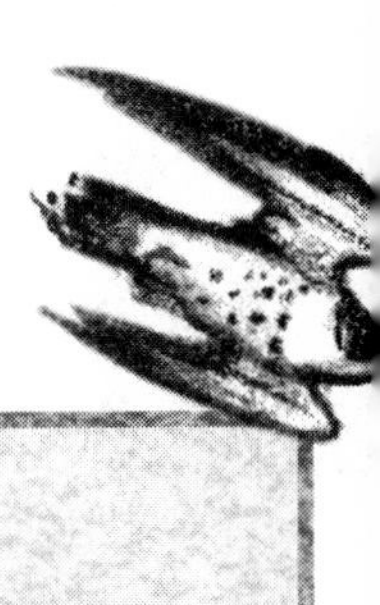

MILES PER HOUR

Thirty-five

Quinny

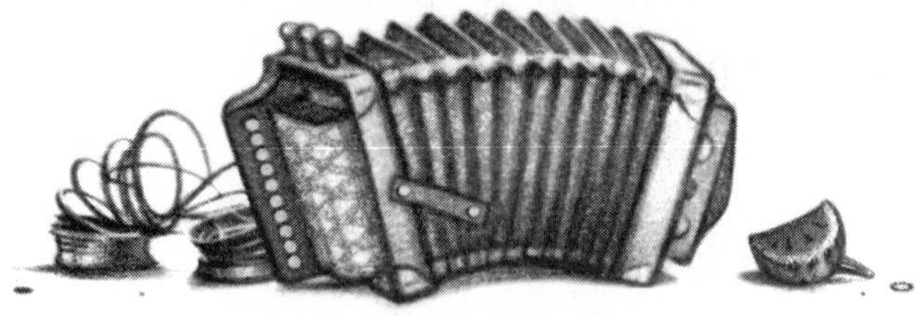

Hopper sits down by my feet.

"Quinny, are you okay?"

I can't talk and cry at the same time, so I just point to the marker stains on my backpack and hold up my bare wrist.

He pulls a tissue out from his backpack and hands it to me. My nose is leaking, but I don't want Hopper's tissue. I don't want anything from that boy. So I get up and push past him and walk out to the school bus, like I'm supposed to.

On the bus, I stare out the window and ignore Hopper some more, which is hard to do since he's sitting right next to me and his looking-looking eyes look especially X-ray-ish.

"Quinny, say something."

But I can't.

The whole ride home I just can't.

I can't trust Hopper anymore. I thought he was my friend, but then he threw me away and I don't even know why. As I sit next to him like this, all I feel is lonely.

Thirty-six

Hopper

I was the one who was supposed to have a bad first day of school, not Quinny. How did things get so mixed up? She won't even look at me.

The bus turns onto our street. Her dad and my mom are waiting for us on the corner.

"Quinny," I call as she walks off the bus and toward her house. "Quinny, wait!"

My words come out louder than I expected.

Quinny stops. She looks back at me with a blank, droopy face.

Now I feel embarrassed and stuck. I don't know what to say next. All the things I am thinking get jumbled up in my mouth—*I'm sorry, I wish we were still friends, I was scared, I was stupid, I didn't mean to ruin everything.*

"What happened to Freya?" I finally blurt out.

Quinny looks surprised by this question. Her shoulders make a sad shrug.

"Freya died of loneliness."

"What?"

"Or a hawk snatched her up."

"You don't know that for sure."

"You're right. It could have been a possum—"

"Quinny—"

"I don't care anyway. Just leave me alone. Who cares about some stupid old chicken?"

And then she walks away.

I stare after her for a moment. Then I follow my mom home.

I go up to my room and shut the door.

I feel like crying, but instead I sit on my bed and think.

I try to think like a chicken.

It doesn't take me long to realize what I have to do this afternoon. And it's not homework.

I walk downstairs and out to our garage. I

find Mom's snorkeling mask and put it on. I find a pair of gardening gloves. From my yard, I pick up the heaviest rock that I can carry.

I walk over to Mrs. Porridge's house and knock on her door. She opens up and looks down at me like I just kicked her.

"What now?" she snaps.

I take a deep breath (which is hard to do when you're wearing a snorkeling mask) and look up at Mrs. Porridge.

"I need a favor."

Thirty-seven

Quinny

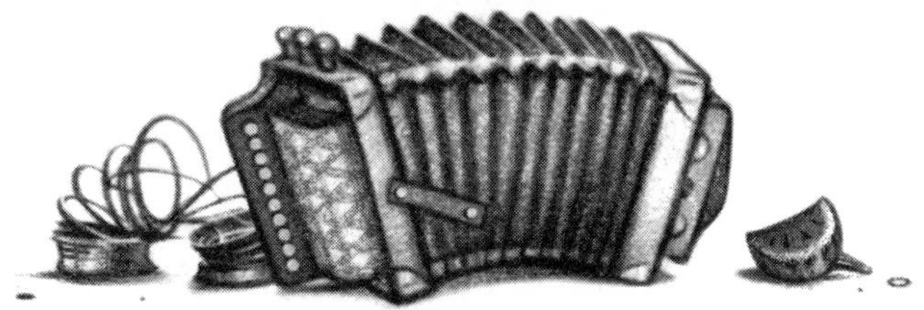

I'm so tired from my terrible first day of school that I run upstairs and crawl under the covers and squeeze my eyes shut. I'm never ever getting out of bed again—ever!

But then I hear clucking in my dreams. It's very familiar clucking, and it's getting wilder and crazier, and it finally wakes me up, which is when I realize that the clucking is REAL, and it's coming from outside my window.

"Freya?!"

"Bockbockbockbockbock!"

I don't see her anywhere out there, so I rush downstairs and run outside, and somehow my feet start running toward all that invisible clucking, and I end up by Hopper's back porch, and then Hopper bursts out from that little trapdoor *under* the porch, and he's got Freya in his arms, all feathery and flapping and dusty and alive!

"Freya! It's you, it's you! And you're not dead!"

I had no idea that chicken was living under Hopper's back porch!

"Hopper, be careful! She looks upset."

"No kidding."

"How on earth did you catch her?"

"Hand-to-hand combat."

"What?"

"I had some help from Mrs. Porridge, too."

Hopper lets go of Freya, and she plops down on the ground and shakes out her feathers, but she can't run away, because she is wearing a spiffy red leash. And I've seen that leash before.

"Is that . . . ?"

"Walter's cat leash," Hopper says. "Mrs. Porridge lent it to me."

"I can't believe Freya let you put her on a leash!"

"Well, she didn't exactly let me," says Hopper. "I wore goggles so she couldn't peck my eyes out. I wore gloves so she wouldn't scratch my hands. And I blocked the door from the inside with a rock, so she couldn't escape from under the porch."

"Hopper, I had no idea you were so brave."

"Me neither. Here, hold the leash," he tells me. "Grandpa Gooley said he would drive us to Mr. McSoren's new place if we caught Freya, so I better go call him."

And then Hopper hands me that chicken on a leash!

"Freya, I missed you so much!" I lean down to her. "You look fabulous in red. This leash matches your wattle."

"BOCKbock," Freya thanks me.

"I'm so glad a fox didn't eat you. Let's go for a stroll."

I pull Freya along—gentle, gentle. "Come on, girl."

"BOCK bock BOCK bockbockbock BOCK."

"I know you don't want to, but just for a little bit, okay?"

I wrap the leash around my hand twice as I walk that gorgeous zebra-chicken down the street. And she actually almost lets me! We're getting the hang of this.

Hopper catches up to us and says, "Grandpa Gooley's on his way."

And then I think of something even more shocking than the fact that I am walking a chicken on a leash. "Hey, Hopper, guess what! You're being nice to me again!"

He shrugs at this.

"But I thought you stopped being my friend."

"I never stopped," he says.

"But you were rude to me and sent me away and yelled, 'Everything's over.'"

"Because I was scared you wouldn't be my friend in school. And then you started playing with Victoria."

Then he tells me about his friend Owen. And how Owen moved away. And how no other friends popped up after that. Until me. And how he was afraid he would lose me, too.

"Hopper, you're such a silly goose. You're never going to lose me as long as you live."

"I'm sorry," he says.

"It's okay, I forgive you."

"And I forgive you, for trying to kiss me," he says.

"I did not! Gross! I never want to kiss you as long as I live."

"Good. Me neither."

"Good. It's a deal."

I reach out and flick his ear, which is one of his three most ticklish places. "Did you know that *butterfly* has the word *butt* in it?" I ask him.

Before Hopper can answer, Grandpa Gooley pulls up in his car. Freya's not too happy that we make her get inside it. That's because she doesn't know where we're taking her.

"Bockbockbock BOCK BOCK BOCK!"

"It's a surprise, Freya. Calm your engine down."

"BOCK bockbockbock BOCK bock BOCK!"

"You'll thank me later," I tell her.

"Everybody *bock*led up?" asks Grandpa Gooley from behind the wheel.

Everybody except the chicken.

We're about to drive off when Mrs. Porridge opens the car door and slides in.

"Don't look so surprised," she huffs at Grandpa Gooley. "Somebody's got to make sure you take proper care of these children."

We finally get going, and Freya spends the whole car ride glaring at us and crabby-clucking. I try to feed her some cheese doodles, but she's not interested.

"Almost there, girl. Almost there." I calm her ruffled feathers.

Finally we pull up to Mr. McSoren's sister's house. She comes out to welcome us, but Freya is so excited to be out of the car she drags me right past her.

"I can't believe you caught that chicken," she says. "Herbert will be so thrilled. He's out back."

Mr. Herbert McSoren is sitting in a wheelchair, facing the backyard. He looks old. He looks tired. He looks lonely. And that's just the back of him. Freya *bock-bock*s and flap-flaps her feathery wings and hops right onto this old guy's lap.

In Mr. McSoren's arms, she's like a new person. Her beady little eyes are shining and her feathers are all fluffed up. I know a happy chicken when I see one. Mr. McSoren looks happy, too. I think he's even crying a bit.

"How can I ever thank you, little girl?" he says to me.

"You just did. And my name's not little girl. It's Quinny Bumble, and I live in your old house, and I'm very, very, extra-very glad to meet you. And this is Hopper. He's the one who actually caught your chicken with tons of courage and Walter's cat leash, which is a long story. By the way, here's a tissue."

Mr. McSoren wipes his eyes. Freya tries to eat the tissue. Then Mr. McSoren's sister cooks everybody some dinner (not chicken). She even puts out a bowl of mealworms for Freya. Then Mr. McSoren gets out his harmonica and plays

"Yankee Doodle Dandy," and everybody dances. Especially me and Freya!

"Go, Freya, go!" I swing my excited hair around, I wiggle my silly-string arms and giggle my clucky-plucky voice and imitate that zebra-chicken's bouncy little steps.

Hopper watches me. I dance extra chickenly to make him laugh.

Then Grandpa Gooley taps my arm. It's time to go home.

But it takes me a long time to stop dancing and start leaving.

"Hurry on up," grumps Mrs. Porridge. "I don't have all night, you know."

Finally I finish saying good-bye to Mr. McSoren and that wonderful bird.

"So long, Freya. Be good."

"Bock," she sighs, all resty and cuddled up on her best friend's lap.

Thirty-eight

Hopper

The ride home is much quieter without Freya's clucking. Much darker, too. The sun is going down fast.

I look over at Quinny sitting next to me in the backseat of Grandpa Gooley's car. Her face is turned away, and her dimples are hiding. She looks tired.

"Quinny? Are you asleep?"

"No more Freya," she says in a voice that's smaller and softer than her regular voice.

"Freya's happy now," I tell her. "She's safe."

"I'm going to miss her," sighs Quinny.

"Oh, snap out of it," says Mrs. Porridge. "That chicken didn't even like you."

“We all had a wonderful time today,” says Grandpa Gooley. “I bet Mr. McSoren will invite us back to visit soon.”

Grandpa Gooley’s right. So why does Quinny seem so sad? She turns to me with a worried look and asks, “Is there a backpack store around here somewhere?”

“A what?”

“Cleo scribbled on my backpack. Victoria said it’s ruined and I have to get a new one.”

“Are you referring to my grand-niece Victoria?” asks Mrs. Porridge.

“Grandpa Gooley, please can we stop?” Quinny begs. “Is there a store that sells back-packs on the way home?”

Grandpa Gooley gives us a confused look in the rearview mirror. I look back at him and tell him with my eyes: I’ll handle this.

“Quinny, it’s kind of late,” I say.

“Please, you don’t understand,” she cries. “I can’t show up at school tomorrow with that ugly, ruined backpack! Victoria’s going to be so mean.”

"I'll have a little talk with that young lady," snaps Mrs. Porridge.

"No, don't! She's already mad I lost her itchy-pink friendship bracelet—"

"Quinny, you don't need a new backpack," I tell her. "Who cares what Victoria thinks?"

"Everyone! All the friends belong to her. She won't let me have any unless I do what she says."

"Not all the friends belong to her," I remind her. "I don't."

Quinny's face calms down a little. "I guess you're right."

She tries to smile at me, but beneath the smile she still looks worried. And tired. "I wish we didn't have school tomorrow," she murmurs as her eyes close.

Pretty soon Quinny starts snoring. Her head droops onto my shoulder and stays there, all big and heavy and noisy. But her hair smells like peaches. It feels soft against my cheek.

Then her arm flops over onto my side of the seat. The back of her hand brushes against my wrist. Just her knuckles. Just a little.

This is how we ride the rest of the way home.

I look down at those two hands, hers and mine. It's not like I'm holding a girl's hand or anything. It's just Quinny, and we're barely touching. And she's asleep, so she won't even remember it.

But it makes me remember how it felt to hold Mom's hand when I was little. It felt good. It felt safe. It felt like I was not alone.

I don't know exactly what's going to happen in school tomorrow.

But I know one thing for sure. I can't let Quinny down again.

Thirty-nine

Quinny

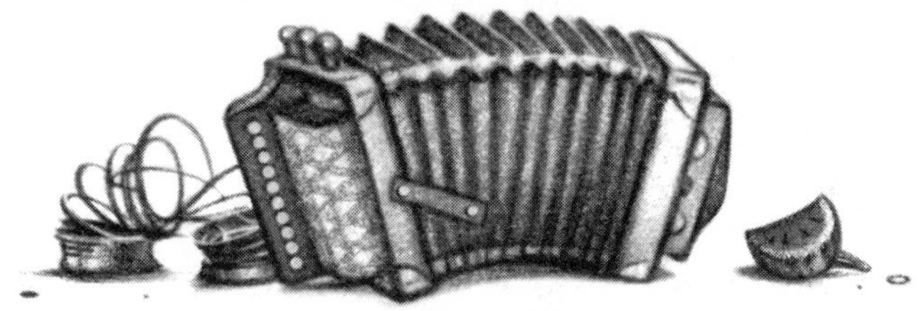

“Quinny, wake up. Let’s get moving.”

But I like it here under the covers, all safe and warm and cozy.

“Quinny, you’re going to miss that school bus.”

I hope so.

“Quinny, chop-chop! I mean it. I don’t have time to drive you. Get up!”

Mom’s voice is an annoying buzzy-bug in my ear, so I finally sit up. But I slept so long that it’s REALLY LATE o’clock now, so I have to rush-brush my teeth and get dressed in a flash and speed-chew my French toast and dodge Piper’s sneaky-spitty fingers and pull on my sneakers and stuff my lunch box into my ugly, ruined backpack. Except I can't even find that backpack.

I look all around the kitchen. "Mom, where's my ugly, ruined backpack?"

Mom's in the middle of feeding Cleo her breakfast mush. "Did you look everywhere?"

I did. I looked everywhere. I look everywhere some more. Just when I'm about to give up and blame Piper for hiding my backpack, I finally spot it.

It's sitting right by our front door, where I didn't even leave it yesterday.

That's weird. What's my backpack doing over there? I walk over to grab it, and then I notice something shocking.

Something very, very, extra-very shocking.

My backpack is not just a backpack anymore. It is now a masterpiece. Cleo's scribbles have turned into people and trees and houses. There's my family and our barn-house, there's Hopper and our soccer-net hammock, there's Mrs. Porridge in her garden with

Walter, plus there's Freya wearing a leash! And guess who is holding that leash!

My backpack looks like my neighborhood now. It looks like my life. My real life.

I pick it up and burst out the front door and run over to the bus stop and throw my arms around Hopper. "Oh, Hopper, thank you, thank you! It's beautiful!"

"I can't breathe," Hopper mumbles from inside my excited, grateful hug.

"Sorry." I let go of him and watch him breathe. "Thanks for saving my backpack."

"No big deal," he says. "I just finished what Cleo started."

But it *is* a big deal. Looking at this fabulous backpack makes me feel good again. It makes me feel strong and special. I smile at Hopper. He almost smiles back at me.

Then the bus comes and we get on it.

During the ride to school, I wonder what's going to happen with Victoria today.

But I don't have to wonder for long. As soon as I get off that bus, she comes up to me.

"Look what I found on the playground," Victoria says, holding up my broken friendship bracelet. I wait for her to apologize, because now she knows I didn't take it off on purpose. But instead she says, "You know, Quinny, you shouldn't be so careless with the presents people give you."

For some strange reason, Victoria's nasty words don't bother me anymore. I turn away from her and walk over to the playground fence.

As I walk, I think about all of her third-grade rules.

I decide I'm going to play tag at recess.

And then I'm going to sit with Hopper at lunch.

I decide I'm going to take a bath with Piper tonight, because I still love baths. Then I'll read us a picture book (at least until she tries to lick me). And then I'll paint my nails green. All twenty of them.

I decide that Victoria Porridge is not my BFF. She might not even be my F. I'll have to wait and see how it goes.

On the other side of the playground fence,

I find my watermelon barrette on the ground, right where Victoria threw it yesterday. I wipe the dirt off that fabulous thing and snap it back into my hair, where it belongs. Finally my head feels like its normal self again.

"Whatever," Victoria says. "That barrette is not even pink."

"That's what I told you before." I say it nicely. I won't be mean to her just because she was mean to me. (But maybe I can make her feel guilty for being mean in the first place.)

Then Victoria finally notices my backpack. She doesn't say it's ruined anymore. She doesn't say it's ugly.

Some other girls come over and look at it. Some boys, too.

One of the girls says, "Wow."

One of the boys says, "Cool."

I take a deep, happy breath and glance at the kid standing next to me. The one with the careful, quiet mouth and those big, looking-looking eyes.

I tell everybody, "My friend Hopper is an artist."

Forty

Hopper

Summer's over.

The second day of school is over, and everything has changed.

Well, almost everything.

Forty-one

Quinny

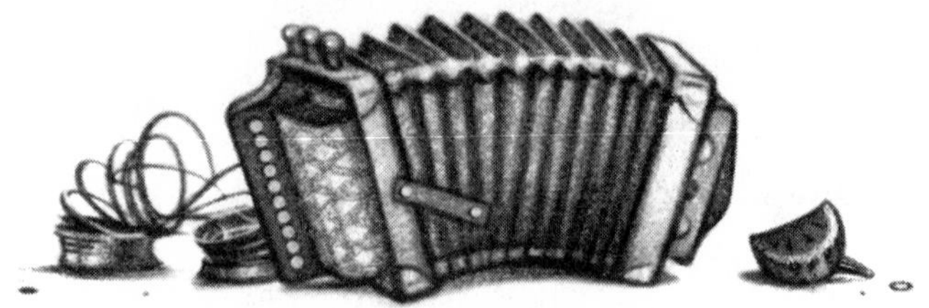

But wait, there's more!

A few weeks later, Hopper and I get home from school one day, and there's a letter in the mail from Mr. McSoren, and it's addressed to BOTH of us, and we tear it open, and it says:

Dear Quinny & Hopper,

I cannot thank you enough for reuniting me with my beloved Freya. She is so happy here and has even made some new friends. As a token of my gratitude, I'm sending a couple of small gifts, via Mrs. Porridge. Please be on the lookout for

Just then, Mrs. Porridge shows up, and she's carrying a big box and inside the box are:

Two chirping chickens!

Little, fluffy, beaky mini-chickens . . . both with stylish black and white zebra stripes!

"It seems that birdbrained bag of feathers has been busy," says Mrs. Porridge.

"You mean these little guys are really Freya's chicken-kids?" I ask. "And they're really for us?"

"No, they're for the president of the United States," says Mrs. Porridge.

I stare at those sweet little zebra-chickens—they're too beautiful to fit into words.

"But aren't they going to miss their mother?" asks Hopper.

"They're not babies anymore," I remind him. "And they have each other."

"Where are we going to keep them?" he asks. "How will we take care of them?"

Hopper and I look at each other. Then we look at Mrs. Porridge.

"Oh no," huffs Mrs. Porridge. "Absolutely not! I have no idea how to build a chicken coop, and I certainly don't have the time. Who needs the pain in the neck of raising smelly, squawky chickens anyway? If you ask me, they're more trouble than they're worth. . . ."

But Mrs. Porridge is smiling.

Acknowledgments

First, the grown-ups: I'm grateful to Quinlan Lee at Adams Literary for believing this heartfelt pile of words was actually a book, and to Laura Schreiber, Tyler Nevins, and Christine Ma at Disney-Hyperion for turning it into such a charming one. Thanks to Daniel Brad, Julie Flanagan Lind, Kirsten Anderson Segal, Sarah Blustain, and Alison Formento for helpful advice on early drafts. I owe my husband, Glen, and mother, Julie, a debt of gratitude for their loving support, and for putting up with my writerly ways.

Now for the kids: A big thank you to Nic Chang, Aidan Dowell, Zoe Gelsi, Veronica Holtz, Jules & Flora Max, Curran Schestag, and, last but not least, my fiercely opinionated daughters Madeline & Julia Schanen. All your feedback helped me revise, revise, revise (and then revise some more). For the inspiration that sparked this story, I'd also like to thank: Faye's voice, Christine's social energy, Julia's artistry and speed, Spencer's enormous heart, Luke & Ethan's bare feet, Eli's way with silence, Madeline's interesting hair and exuberant smile, Torger's deep well of emotion and intelligence, Lily's chickens, and Lucas O.'s great big looking-looking eyes. I look forward to watching you all grow and soar in the years ahead.